A SIMPLE COUNTRY KILLING

BLYTHE BAKER

～

Death, and Helen Lightholder, return to Brookminster with the murder of the village vicar. As Helen investigates the ghastly crime, she soon finds herself a suspect of the local police. To clear her name and protect her friends, Helen must discover the truth and outwit a devious killer.

But Helen's personal life is not without its own mysteries and one of them continues to stalk her in the shadows...

～

1

Upon my return from London, I found myself far more exhausted than I ever thought I could be.

It was early in the morning, a Monday in the middle of August. I had been in the capitol city for eight days, staying with Patrick and Lily Gordon once again while officer after officer filtered through their home, seeking out the information I had brought with me.

Everyone, including Patrick and Lily, was astounded when I told them that I had been the one to kill Sidney, who I learned was indeed using a false name. His real name was Helmut Reinhart, and he had been on the run ever since Roger was killed.

One night, as a rainstorm rattled the windows of the Gordon's townhome, a man named General Klein, someone that Roger and Patrick both served under, pulled me into Patrick's study where we could discuss the matter in private. He stood at the window, peering out into the stormy night, chewing on the end of his mahogany smoking pipe.

"I imagine that you know the truth now. The *real* truth, I mean. About Roger's death," he said.

I stared cautiously at his back, my mind racing. "I... believe so."

There were three realities of Roger's death. First, there was the article released in the papers after his death, claiming he had been killed in an air raid bombing. Until just about a month ago, that was how I believed he had died.

Second, there was the story that he had been killed by a German spy who he had discovered infiltrating the ranks of the British army, a man who had later sought after me for secret information that Roger had slipped to me unknowingly.

And third...there was the *real* truth, the truth that maybe only one or two people knew.

Roger was actually alive, and he'd been spending the months since his supposed death fulfilling secret and dangerous missions for the government. At least, that was what I assumed he was doing. I hadn't spoken to him myself, but he had made himself known to me just before I left for London, revealing that he had been the mysterious silhouette I had seen many times in the shadows, watching after me.

General Klein turned and looked at me, smoke billowing from his pipe. "Are you certain?" he asked.

Unsure whether he was one of the few who knew Roger was still alive, I kept my mouth shut. I wasn't going to be the one to reveal that information. As far as everyone else was still aware, Roger was dead, and I had to play along with that until he made it clear otherwise, for my own protection, as well as his own.

Klein was a foreboding man, with his thick moustache

and hard gaze that had seen far too much warfare. "Well..." he said. "I'm sorry it all turned out this way. We realize you are just as much a victim as he was."

Those cryptic words told me nothing, but I knew he couldn't very well reveal to me that Roger was alive when there were very likely ears directly on the other side of the door who would overhear. And that would surely compromise Roger's mission.

A glimmer of something serious flickered in Klein's gaze, and in that moment, I knew he meant to tell me that Roger was alive.

"I do know the truth, Sir," I said. "Every bit of it."

General Klein nodded. "Very well. Your country thanks you for your service, Helen Lightholder. And for that of your husband, delivering the code key to you in such a way, knowing it would be kept safe. My only regret is that you had to suffer through the difficulties that Helmut Reinhart brought on you. I imagine this experience has been troubling."

Troubling was a very mild way of putting it.

Lily Gordon insisted that I stay with them while I recover from the shock of Sidney – Helmut's – attack, but I told her I was needed back at home. "Besides, he's gone now. I don't have to be frightened of him any longer."

And I believed that. I didn't have to be frightened of him living right next door, or his ability to kill me whenever he pleased. He was no longer alive...but that didn't mean he didn't live on in my nightmares, which came every time I closed my eyes at night.

They weren't strange nightmares. They were not filled with bizarre twists and turns, nor were they confusing. I didn't have to run anywhere, and things weren't hidden behind locked doors, as most of my nightmares with Roger had been.

It was as if my mind had captured that moment when I killed Sidney and permanently recorded it in my memory to play over, and over, and over. As such, my nights were rarely filled with sleep anymore. Instead, I would lie awake, reading, trying to distract myself from the dreams that seemed to taunt me from just beyond the veil of sleep.

Returning home to Brookminster was both a great blessing and a bit of a worry. As the first light of dawn appeared over the hills outside the village, I stood at my door, staring up at the house that had become so much of a strange place to me since I had moved in.

Unwillingly, my eyes shifted to the house next door.

It looked much colder than it ever had before. Once, it brought a smile to my face. It was the place where a friend lived, someone who had proved himself trustworthy time and time again. The front garden was a place where many good conversations had been had, where laughs had been shared, where my heart had been warmed and comforted.

Sidney Mason had been a wonderful person in my life... and it broke my heart to realize that he was never real in the first place.

I unlocked my door and stepped inside, where I found everything in my shop just as I had left it.

My eyes drifted toward the back door, where Sidney would so often come to see me, knocking on the window and peering inside, waving at me while wearing that charming grin of his. He would offer to fix the squeak in my door, or the sticking drawer in one of my window displays, or the wobbly leg on my dining table. But it wasn't just me.

He would offer the same to anyone who needed help. He was a good man.

But it was all to get to me. To find information about Roger. To ultimately find the letters that Roger had written to me, and then to destroy them so the information couldn't be transmitted back to his superiors.

Sidney had died thinking he'd won, when in reality, I'd memorized the letter that Roger had written to me, the important one, the one that held the precious code key that Sidney had been so bent on destroying.

I dragged my suitcase upstairs, already feeling exhausted. I had yet to get any sleep that night, having been awake in order to catch the train that left London so early in the morning.

I collapsed onto the bed, not even having the energy to remove my jacket. I grabbed my pillow, drawing it toward me, and pulling my legs up toward my middle, and quickly fell asleep.

I woke with a start, what felt like just a few minutes later...only to find that it was very nearly dark again, and the amber light of sunset was flickering through the opposite windows of my little flat.

I pulled myself out of bed, my limbs aching and stiff from lying in the same position for so long, and wandered over to the window.

It was nearly dusk. I'd slept the whole day...without having another terrible nightmare.

I rubbed my eyes, my lashes sticking together with sleep.

There was no sense in staying in. I would likely not sleep through the night now.

I should have set an alarm...I thought bitterly.

I had no fresh groceries, no milk, nothing to readily eat, and my stomach growled with hunger pangs.

It was best if I went out to find something to eat, even something small to just tide me over until the morning when I could find my ration coupons and go get my allotted groceries for the week.

I knew the pub would be open, but after Sidney's fiasco there, I had no interest in that place. The inn might be a better choice, though the last time I had been there had been with Sam Graves, and I wondered if the owners might have thought it had been a romantic engagement.

I changed my jacket, ran a brush through my hair, and made my way out to the street in order to find something to eat.

The roads were peppered with puddles, and water droplets clung to the ends of the branches of the trees. Somehow I'd managed to sleep through the rainstorm, as well.

Streetlights flickered to life as I passed beneath them, filling the street with a warm glow. The clouds were puffy and dark overhead like a blanket over the village.

I breathed in the fresh air, the scent of the rain still present. It was one of the things I loved most about Brookminster. London's air was smoky, coated the lungs, and sometimes even smelled foul, as if something had died within the walls of the nearby buildings.

It was not so here, though. Brookminster was such a different place.

I came upon the center of town, on High Street, and headed toward the inn, when the low, stone wall of the church appeared. I followed alongside it, the church sitting atop the hill as it always did, made of beautiful, pale stone. It was quiet now, at this hour. The vicar, Mr. James, was likely to be at home now with his wife, enjoying the coolness of the evening.

The cemetery was peaceful, as well, which was a relief. The stones all rested in their rows, shadowed in the fading light. For a brief moment, I considered stepping inside and seeking out the grave of the Polish refugee who had been killed recently, just to pay my respects.

I can pay my respects tomorrow, when my stomach is full and I am not hurrying to beat the setting of the sun.

I kept walking, the gate of the cemetery coming into sight...when I thought I heard a voice.

"...lp...m..."

I stopped, straining my ears. I was standing in the middle of a busy street, after all. Many families were likely preparing their children for bed. Some of the little ones might still be out playing in the back garden, enjoying their last few minutes of freedom before their mothers dragged them in for a bath or for their evening story.

And I did hear children, along with other voices. A group of people down the street were leaving the inn, one man throwing back his head and laughing. A woman stood out in her garden, speaking with another woman, though their voices were so low I likely wouldn't have heard them had I been walking beside them.

That wasn't the voice I heard, though, I said to myself. *It seemed more –*

And then I heard it again.

"...Help...me..."

My stomach dropped to my feet.

Not again. Oh, please...not again.

2

I stood frozen to the spot, my heart pounding in my chest. Had I really heard someone calling for help?

No...that couldn't be. Not when the rest of the world around me was as pleasant and as calm as it was. Birds were singing their last songs for the day, retiring to their nests tucked away in the limbs of the nearby trees. A couple made their way down the street on their bicycles, likely ready for a comfortable, relaxing night in. Lights began to shine in the upper windows of the ivy-strewn homes down High Street, preparing for the first of the stars to flicker to life in the dark sky overhead.

I glanced over my shoulder into the cemetery. I was just hearing things, wasn't I?

I haven't been getting much sleep...and goodness knows I have been living in a mindset where everything that could possibly go wrong will. It is more than likely that I am just hearing things, and my mind is trying to play tricks on me.

That was it. It had to be. I was not ready to accept that I

had, indeed, been hearing someone crying out for help. Especially not from the church cemetery.

I took a step, my attention already redirecting itself toward the inn, ready for my meal.

But a clear sound of coughing made me stop once again, along with an agonized cry of pain.

My stomach turned to ice.

I realized I could keep walking. It was not my responsibility to stop and make sure that whoever it was who was crying out was all right. How did I know it wasn't just a group of older children, playing among the tombstones?

That wasn't my only option, either. I could go and find help.

I turned and gazed into the cemetery, my eyes searching for any sign of distress. I found none, though; everything seemed as it always was.

*I can't leave them...*I thought. *If I do, I might be too late when I get back. Perhaps I could help. Maybe it's nothing more than a twisted ankle, or perhaps a bump on the head.*

Steeling my nerves, I knew that I couldn't just walk away. It wouldn't be right.

I turned back to the gate and stepped through, into the cool, darkness of the cemetery.

"Hello?" I called out as I followed along the worn, dirt path that wound its way through the graves. "Is someone there?"

"He – help – "

The voice was slightly louder, and it sounded familiar, though I couldn't quite put my finger on who it belonged to.

"Keep talking," I said, picking up the pace.

"Here..."

I made a sharp right turn, following along the wrought

iron fence that ran alongside the street. Beyond, I saw an older woman walking her greying terrier, which was happily sniffing at the air, his tongue lolling out.

I heard coughing once again, just a short ways from the edge of the fence. How had no one else heard it?

I came around the trunk of an ancient elm tree, and gasped as I saw the body of Mr. James slumped against it, clutching at his stomach...his fingers glistening with fresh, ruby red blood.

"Mr. James," I said, kneeling beside the vicar, resting my hand on his shoulder to steady him. "Mr. James, can you hear me?"

The sharp tang of blood reached my nose, metallic and strong in the cool, summer air. It made my stomach coil into knots.

The thin man slowly lifted his chin up toward me. It had only been a fortnight since I'd seen him last, but his face, now gaunt, seemed almost unrecognizable. The usual smile and kindness in his eyes were replaced with a pained grimace, and clouded vision.

"Hel...Helen..." he mumbled, his breathing shallow and labored.

"What happened to you?" I asked.

His head lolled to the side, exposing some of the greying hair on his dark head near his temples.

"Mr. James, stay with me," I said, gently shaking him. "You need to stay awake. I can go get you help, but you need to stay awake, all right?"

He struggled to look at me once again, his green eyes hazy behind his tortoiseshell glasses.

"He...he hated me," Mr. James said, then sputtered.

Blood spattered from the edge of his mouth, dotting the front of his shirt as well as mine. "Never...meant to – "

He was losing too much blood. I moved the front of his jacket and found the whole front of his shirt stained, with a dark, gleaming spot just below his ribs the size of a sixpence. One of his lungs must have been punctured.

"It's all right," I said. "If you just hold on for a few minutes, I can go find you some help, and we can get you to the doctor, get you all patched up – "

With surprising strength, he grabbed onto my arm, pulling me back down toward him.

His eyes were wide with desperation, and as he opened his mouth to speak, he coughed, more blood mingling with his spittle. "No..." he said. "I know to – to whom I go..."

"Who did this to you?" I asked.

Mr. James shook his head. "His anger – he said he never could let me – I tried to – tried to – " He gasped for air, sputtering once again, his body swaying.

I reached out to help steady him. My hands found warm stickiness against his chest...which made my stomach twist.

I knew I couldn't leave him. As he coughed, his entire body trembled. His face had lost all color, and the pink spots coating his lips proved to me that even if someone were to get here in time, he likely wouldn't survive being carried away from this spot. The movement alone would probably kill him.

I quickly pulled the sweater I wore from my shoulders, and rolling it into a ball, pressed it against his chest. "Here, keep pressure on the wound," I said, realizing my own hands were shaking terribly. "It'll help stop the bleeding."

Mr. James, gasping for air, didn't respond. He leaned his head back against the tree.

"I'm...not afraid...of death," he said in a voice barely above a whisper.

My eyes stung with tears as I stared at him, the last of the sunlight dipping behind the rolling hills in the distance. Wind rushed through the boughs of the elm tree above our heads.

He had only ever been kind to me. Kind to everyone. Honorable, righteous, and compassionate. He spent his free hours helping those in the village, caring for the sick, visiting the poor. He taught wonderful sermons every Sunday morning, and it was clear from speaking with him for just a moment how much he loved what he did, and how strong and how deep his faith was.

"Maybe it's not your time to go yet," I said, feeling entirely helpless and desperately sad at the same time.

His breathing was more of a wheeze than a true breath. He stared up toward the heavens. "No..." he said. "This – this was not the way I thought I might – might – "

A gurgling sound erupted from his throat, and his muscles in his shoulder began to twitch.

Unable to stand it any longer, I stood and hurried around the tree, waving my blood-stained hands above my head as I made my way toward the fence.

"Help!" I cried. "It's the vicar! He's – he's dying!"

A few faces in the street turned toward me. I recognized them all. Mrs. Georgianna. Mr. and Mrs. Trent. Mr. Hodgins, the butcher.

Mrs. Georgianna let out a terrible shriek of terror when she saw me, and turned, fleeing down the street as fast as her legs would carry her.

"Someone has hurt him!" I cried, grasping the bars of

the fence as I peered out into the street. "Please, someone go get the police! Get a doctor!"

Another woman down the opposite side of the street screamed as well, which was followed by another some distance away.

Mr. Trent and Mr. Hodgins looked at one another, and without a word, hurried toward the gate leading into the cemetery.

Mrs. Trent, however, stood there, stunned...staring blankly at me, her hand clutched over her heart.

"The police!" someone further down the road shouted. "Fetch the Inspector!"

"And a doctor," I cried. "And hurry!"

I turned and hurried back through the tombstones toward Mr. James, the blood singing in my ears.

I stumbled, nearly catching my ankle on an exposed root that was protruding up through the ground. I grabbed onto one of the graves, using it to right myself as I continued to run toward him.

Mr. Hodgins and Mr. Trent were bending over Mr. James by the time I arrived.

"We need to – " I began to say.

"It's too late," Mr. Hodgins said darkly, glaring at me. "He's already dead."

"What?" I asked, icy fear flooding my veins.

I knelt down beside Mr. James, laying my hands on his shoulder.

"No..." I said. "He was just – he was just speaking with me. Maybe he's only lost consciousness – "

I reached out to touch his face, but a hand grabbed onto my wrist, preventing me.

"Why do you have blood all over your hands?"

Mr. Hodgins was glaring down at me, and Mr. Trent looked troubled behind him.

"I was – I was helping him," I said. "I heard him calling out for help, and I just found him like this – "

Mr. Hodgins yanked me up to my feet as easily as if I were a child. His gaze hardened. "And how do you explain the blood on your blouse?"

I looked down and saw the spatters of blood on my front. "He – he was coughing. I think his lung must have been punctured. You can see it in the corner of his mouth – "

"Don't lie to me..." Mr. Hodgins said. "I've worked with animals and blood long enough to know how easy it is to be sprayed when you are the one doing the slicing in the first place."

My stomach flipped over. "You think I did this?"

Mr. Trent was getting to his feet, having knelt down beside Mr. James. "This sweater..." he said, looking up at me, the bloody mess cradled gently in his hands. "Is this yours, Helen?"

My mouth had suddenly gone dry. "I didn't do this," I said, shaking my head. "Surely you cannot be serious in thinking I would have – "

Mr. Hodgins' grip around my wrist tightened. "And yet, all the evidence seems to point right toward you. Who happened to be here when he died? You. Who has blood all over herself? You do."

"No," I said. "I came here to help. I wanted to save him – "

"You've been sticking your nose into all of these murders happening around the village," Mr. Hodgins said, a slight growl to his words. "And I'm starting to think you had more to do with them then you have been letting on."

My heart pounded against my chest, and I struggled to free myself from his grip. It was startling to me that a normally fair minded man like Mr. Hodgins could turn so suddenly nasty. "N – no," I said, leaning away from him, the sharp scent of the blood hanging in the air around me like a sinister perfume. "I didn't kill anyone. I would never – "

"Helen," Mr. Trent said as gently as he could, sorrow clear in his aged face. "You were here at the scene of the crime. His blood is on your hands. How else do you explain this?"

I could only stare at the man. He really thought I was the one who had done this? "Why is it so hard to believe that I found him here?"

"Did he tell you who killed him?" Mr. Trent asked.

"He was – he was trying to, but he was delirious, and – "

"Don't ask her that," Mr. Hodgins said. "She could very easily just lie to you about it."

"I'm not lying," I said, my eyes narrowing, my hand beginning to throb as Mr. Hodgins clenched it so tightly. "Now if you would kindly release me – "

"So you can run away?" Mr. Hodgins asked. "I don't think so. I'll be taking you down to the police station myself, so everyone can see the blood on your hands. Mr. Trent, would you mind staying with Mr. James?"

"Of course," Mr. Trent said heavily.

"How do we know that he can't still be saved?" I asked, looking down at Mr. James. "If we can get a doctor here, maybe something can be done – "

"There's no pulse," Mr. Trent said, shaking his head. "He's gone."

"And how can we be sure that he wasn't dead long before you came crying down to us in the street?" Mr. Hodgins asked, starting to pull me along the path back toward the front gates of the churchyard. I glared at him as he dragged me along. "Why on earth would I alert you to the body if I had been the one to do it? Wouldn't it have been much wiser if I had just killed him and fled the scene?"

"Or you were hoping to throw everyone off the scent," Mr. Hodgins said. "Why would anyone suspect you if you were the one to just *happen* to stumble upon the body?"

"That clearly didn't stop you from thinking I'd done it..." I muttered.

He gave a merciless shake as he whipped me around the corner of a large tombstone.

We returned to the path leading back down to the street, when Mr. Hodgins stopped.

I looked up...and my heart sank.

Inspector Sam Graves was standing there, glowering at the scene before him.

"Caught her in the act, Sir," Mr. Hodgins said, shoving me toward Sam. "Or at least, just as she was finishing him off."

I staggered to a halt in front of Sam, blowing some of my chestnut hair from my eyes. "Sam, I didn't do this. Please, you have to believe – "

He held up a hand to stop me in midsentence. "Whatever you are going to say, you should save it for later," he said. His tone was flat, and his stare blank. "Thank you, Mr. Hodgins. I can take it from here."

To my horror, I saw Sam produce a pair of handcuffs from somewhere, spinning them around his fingers.

"Just be patient," Sam whispered to me as he stepped around behind me, gently drawing my wrists together. I felt the bite of the cold metal as it touched my wrists. "We will figure all this out."

He snapped the handcuffs in place.

I stared helplessly up at him.

How had this all gone so horribly wrong?

3

I opened my mouth to argue with Sam as he started to lead me from the gates into the churchyard, but he gave me an almost imperceptible shake of his head, silencing me. I was vaguely aware of a pair of constables rushing past us toward the dead man we left behind. Bystanders out on the street must have alerted the police to what had happened.

Sam's grip was firm on my upper arm as he walked me down the street toward the police station. He wasn't nearly as angry about it all as Mr. Hodgins was...which surprised me. As we walked, I had time to recall the butcher's words.

Was that how people in Brookminster saw me? Did they all think I had nothing better to do than get involved in these murders that had been happening since my arrival? Couldn't they understand that somehow, they all had some sort of tie to me?

No, they certainly wouldn't understand that, would they? Not even if I were to explain it to them. They would write it off as an excuse...

My fingers were sticky, the dried portions of blood tugging at the skin around my knuckles as I clenched my fists.

Mr. James...how had he died in those few moments when I'd gone looking for help? And why was everyone so quick to assume it was me?

I couldn't understand.

All the streetlights had flickered into life, bathing the street in a warm glow. It would have been an otherwise peaceful night...had the people walking past us not been reacting the way they were.

Some gasped. Others cried out. Parents drew their children to the other side of the street, covering their eyes. People I considered friends and loyal customers of my shop glared at me, or stared in horror, pale faced and frightened. I realized that I must make a horrible sight, what with all the blood spattered on me.

The police station appeared up ahead, and it couldn't have come soon enough. The whole village seemed to have turned against me in one moment.

Sam was gentle as he walked with me up the stairs. "Now, I should let you know how things are going to proceed from here," he said. "Once we get you through processing, I am going to take you into questioning. If I were you, I would do your best to remain calm, and to answer all of my questions as honestly as possible."

I bit back my retort. Why on earth would I ever be anything less than truthful?

"And if we can...I'll make sure we get you cleaned up at some point," he said.

My heart skipped. That certainly would be preferable.

The police station was much darker than I remembered

it. The lights overhead seemed dim, and the floor seemed cold and unforgiving. There was no color on the walls, and the air smelled of sweat, must, and blood.

Sam steered me clear away from the reception area, and instead led me straight to a grey, metal door that I had never been past before, nor had I ever noticed it, painted the same drab color as the rest of the wall.

Shame clung to me like a shawl as we entered. Not only was I filthy, I knew that everyone out in the front room of the station had seen me, and had likely recognized me. How was I ever going to live down this moment? Even though I was innocent, the glares I'd received told me everything I needed to know about people's confidence in me. Was my reputation here in Brookminster really that fragile?

The room beyond was as dimly light as the foyer, with nothing more than a simple desk area and a row of chairs against the wall.

"Go ahead and have a seat," Sam said, gesturing to the first vacancy in the empty line of cold, metal seats.

I didn't say anything as I did as he asked. It was in my best interest to cooperate, I knew. Any fighting I might want to do instinctively would only get me in worse trouble.

My eyes stung with tears as I settled into the chair, the handcuffs behind me cutting into my flesh.

Sam approached the desk where an older gentleman was sitting, his nose bent over a page of numbers. "Evening, Jim," Sam said. "I've got someone in for questioning."

The man glanced up at him briefly. "Oh? Who is it this time, Terrance again – "

His eyes shifted toward to me, and then widened like saucers.

"Oh, I see," he said, looking me up and down, his gaze lingering on the spatters of blood on the front of my blouse. "Very well, here's the forms."

Sam took them. "Thank you," he said.

He picked out a pen from a cup full of them, and began filling out the forms for the records. *My* record. It made me wonder if Sam already had notes tucked away somewhere about me, or if anyone had come in with a complaint or a false testimony about me.

I looked away, unable to stomach it any longer. How in the world had I gotten here?

When Sidney had attacked me in his home, I had defended myself. Sam had known that, and we hadn't had to go through all these steps. Was it because I'd gone right to him that time? He had never once considered sending me to prison, even though I had been the one to...

I shook my head. It was too difficult to think about right now.

Sam must have felt my gaze on him, because he gave me a sidelong look out of the corner of his eye.

When our gazes met, I noticed a depth to his expression that surprised me. He was trying to tell me something without having to say it. What, though?

His look didn't last long. He turned away, rather sadly, his focus on the papers before him once again.

I wasn't left alone with my thoughts for too much longer. I heard Sam replace the cap on the pen and sigh heavily as he stood upright. "I'm going to take her right in for questioning," he said.

"As you wish," Jim said, giving me a startled look out of the corner of his eye.

Sam picked up a clipboard, and then walked back over to me, a blank expression on his face. "Are you ready?" he asked.

How was I supposed to answer that?

I got to my feet, and he slipped his hand underneath my arm once again, leading me down a dreary hall.

We walked in silence. I agonized over it, wanting desperately for him to say something, anything, that might make the situation a little less frightening. The longer he went without speaking, the worse I began to feel. Was I really going to be blamed for Mr. James' murder? Was this where my luck finally ran out?

He stopped before another bare, metal door, pulling a bundle of keys from deep inside his pockets. Sliding one into the lock on the door, he glanced down at me.

"Just stay calm, all right?" he asked in a low voice, his other hand resting on the door handle. "And remember that everything you say will be overheard by more than just me."

I swallowed, though it was a struggle, given that my throat felt more like a dry stream bed.

He pushed the door open, and my stomach dropped.

It was a type of room that I'd seen before, but I never thought I would have to enter one.

Dreary like the rest of the station, the room was small, with three blank walls, and a fourth where a large, mirrored piece of glass was inlaid.

I caught a glimpse of myself for the first time in its reflection, and the knots in my chest tightened...

The vicar's blood was all over me. Not just sprinkled on the front of my shirt. It had somehow been smeared across my cheek, streaked across my exposed collarbone, and stained the whole front of me to the point where I couldn't be sure that I didn't have a wound underneath it all.

*I see why Mr. Hodgins thought it was me...*I realized with horror.

Sam brought me to the only piece of furniture in the room; a plain metal table with two simple chairs on either side of it.

He sat me down in one chair, and I felt his hands grab my own from behind. My heart skipped, finally thinking things might be all right, especially as he unlocked my handcuffs.

Disappointment returned full force, though, when he brought my hands around to my front, reconnected the cuffs, and attached the cuffs to another metal hook imbedded in the surface of the table. There was no way I was going anywhere.

Sam went to sit at the chair across from me when a door behind me opened, and in the glass window on the wall beside me, I saw two burly officers step into the room. They said nothing as they closed the door behind themselves, leaning against the concrete wall.

Sam glanced at the glass. "Could we get her a wet towel to clean up with?" he asked. "The stench of blood is revolting this late in the evening..."

My stomach fell to the floor. So this was how he was going to treat me, hmm?

He looked over at me, and something in his gaze made me look closer.

He squinted his eyes ever so briefly and there was an almost imperceptible shake of his head.

Was he trying to tell me that he wasn't meaning to be

unkind? Was this the only way that he could get through this while still maintaining his authority?

With the rumors flying around the station that he and I were romantically connected, then it was only natural that he would have to do his best to not show favoritism in any way.

*I suppose I should expect harsh remarks like that one, then...*I thought.

A few moments later, the door opened behind me again, and someone passed something through to one of the officers behind me.

He then walked around to me and tossed the cold, damp towel on my hands.

I looked up at Sam, questioning.

He nodded. "Feel free to clean up what you can, but I still expect you to cooperate with me and listen to my questions."

"Yes, sir," I said, doing what I could to wipe the dried blood off my hands that were locked in the cuffs.

Sam sighed, pulling the clipboard toward him. He flipped to the third page, and I watched as he scrawled my name across the top.

I wonder if he ever thought he'd have to write my name up there...

"All right, Mrs. Lightholder. I'm going to start off by asking you where you were this evening, and what you were doing." He looked up at me, his gaze steady.

I focused on the cool wetness of the towel instead of the fear bubbling up inside of me. "I was at home for most of the evening," I said. "I just returned from London this morning, and as I hadn't slept at all the night before, I spent most of the day in my room, sleeping. I woke just before seven, and found I was rather hungry, so I – "

Sam spun the tip of his pen through the air. "You can skip all of the unimportant information," he said. "What brought you to the cemetery?"

My shoulders hunched. *He's not doing it to be unkind,* I told myself. And I hoped I was right about that. "Well, as I said, I was hungry, and had no food in my house, so I decided to go to the inn for dinner."

Sam's look told me to hurry up.

"And on my way, I was passing by the cemetery, the gate on High Street, when I heard someone crying out for help. For a few moments, I considered coming straight here for help, but I wasn't even sure I had heard it in the first place. So I went in to see if maybe it was nothing more than some children playing among the graves...or if it was someone who was hurt, perhaps nothing more than a person who had fallen or something easy like that," I said.

Sam scrawled down a shortened version of what I'd said. "Very well. What happened then?"

I shifted in the hard, metal chair. My heart rate was quickening, and I dreaded retelling the story again. I wanted to leave nothing out, however, in case it helped to prove that I was not, in fact, the person who killed Mr. James.

"I walked into the cemetery, calling out for whoever was looking for help. I wandered along the fence, not seeing or hearing anything, and then when I came to one of the elm trees just a few meters from the fence, I saw Mr. James lying there against the trunk."

Sam looked up at me, but I couldn't read his thoughts. I hardly ever could. "Go on," he said.

I felt the gaze of the two officers behind me on the back of my head, and knew there must have been people on the other side of the one way mirror.

"I bent down, seeing he was still alive, though barely..." I said. It was as if a hand was gripping my heart, and squeezing it. "I told him to stay awake, and that if he held on for just a few more moments, I could go and get some help..."

"Did he say anything to you?" Sam asked.

I nodded. "He did. He tried to tell me who his killer was. He mentioned something about how 'he' hated him, and how 'he' had been so angry that he couldn't let Mr. James – "

"He?" Sam asked. "That does seem rather convenient for you..."

My eyes narrowed. "He was coughing and losing blood. I'm amazed he was able to get that much out."

Sam sighed, writing down more notes. "You said his wounds were severe?"

"Yes," I said. "There was a large cut in his stomach, just below his ribs. I think whoever did it must have punctured one of his lungs. The blood was all over my front from when he would cough, and the blood would spray everywhere..."

Sam made note. "Did you see a weapon anywhere?"

I shook my head. "No," I said. "No weapon. The constables who went into the churchyard, they'll find my sweater there. I used it to try and stop the bleeding."

Sam muttered something underneath his breath, writing something else down. "And then what?" he asked. "How did Mr. Hodgins and Mr. Trent find you?"

"I ran to the fence, yelling for help," I said. "The vicar was near death, hardly able to keep his focus on me any longer. I couldn't just watch him die there...So when I saw people in the street, I called them over. Mr. Hodgins and Mr. Trent met me where Mr. James was lying, but by the time I got back to his body, he was dead."

Sam nodded his head, but didn't say anything, so I continued.

"They immediately thought that I'd been the one to do it, given the...well, the blood on me," I said, looking down at the now pinkish towel that I still held in my hands. "Mr. Hodgins said that his profession had taught him a thing or two about blood spray, and he accused me of being the one to harm Mr. James in the first place...something about how it had spattered on my blouse. But that wasn't what happened. There is blood on Mr. James' lips, and I'm certain there would have been spray on the ground, as well."

Sam held up a hand, and gave me brief look of warning.

Keep calm, I told myself. *It won't do any good to get worked up and start throwing accusations around.*

Sam finished his notes. "Is there anything else you would like to add?" he asked. "Did you see anyone suspicious around the body? Was there anyone else in the cemetery with you?"

I shook my head. "Not that I saw, no," I said. "It was late for anyone to be in the cemetery, after all."

Sam nodded. "Very well..." he said, rising to his feet. "I was going to keep you overnight for further questioning, but you have been cooperative. I am going to dismiss you under the understanding that you are not allowed to leave Brookminster for any reason during the length of this investigation. Am I clear?"

I stared up into his face, almost dumbfounded. He was going to let me go?

"But Inspector, she's the only suspect," said one of the officers behind me.

"There's no evidence that she's the one who committed the crime," Sam said. "And her prior record shows that she is a law abiding citizen."

The officer behind me clicked his tongue in disagreement.

Soon after, Sam unhooked me from the table, and walked with me from the room.

I looked up at him, wanting to speak, but he shook his head, indicating I should wait.

He didn't unhook the handcuffs until we were standing just outside the police station.

Night had fallen in earnest, and there wasn't another soul out on the street.

I rubbed my raw wrists gratefully, seeing streaks of blood still sticking to my skin that I hadn't been able to reach with the towel. "Thank you..." I said.

Sam sighed. "Helen, I don't know how you got yourself mixed up in this, but I would have thought, by now, that you would have wanted to stay as far away from anything like this as possible."

"Of course that's what I want," I said. "Do you think I went looking for trouble tonight in that churchyard?"

"No," Sam said. "But trouble certainly likes to look for you, doesn't it?"

I stared at the ground, biting the inside of my lip. "You don't think I did it?"

"Of course I don't," Sam said. "I know you wouldn't do something like that. But that doesn't mean the evidence isn't all pointing directly to you right now. The good thing is that I've built up a reputation at this station for being thorough in my investigations, and that I have an eye for whether or not people are telling the truth. There might be some who will question why I let you walk free tonight, but don't let them bother you, all right?"

"What am I supposed to do now, then?" I asked, staring off into the distance, up the street. "Until you find who the real killer is, everyone in the village is going to suspect me."

"I thought that answer would be obvious," Sam said. "You lie low and wait for the police to get to the bottom of this. Having said that, something tells me you're not going to take this advice, are you?"

"It isn't in me to wait for rescue from others," I said. "Anyway, this case is the most personal yet, isn't it?"

"Whatever you do, I hope you'll be careful this time around," he said. "But don't worry, Helen. In the end, we'll clear your name, and salvage your reputation. You have my word."

I believed him, but that didn't make the knots in my chest loosen at all. "I'm sorry I put you in this situation tonight," I said. "I never meant to."

"You don't need to apologize for anything," he said. He looked over his shoulder at the station, and let out a long sigh. "I should get back to the paperwork. And I'm sure the other officers have brought the body in by now. When we have the results from the autopsy, I'll be sure to let you know. Perhaps it will help give you some answers."

"Thank you," I said.

Sam shook his head. "Poor Mr. James...of all the people..."

"I know," I said, and for the first time, I allowed myself a chance to grieve for the man. "I can't imagine why anyone would want to kill him."

"People can be evil," Sam said. "Haven't you learned anything from all the cases these last few months?"

"I know," I said. "But that doesn't mean I have to like that answer."

"No one does," Sam said. "But just because we don't like the truth doesn't mean it isn't just that. The truth."

4

I had no idea what to do next.

I realized the news of what had occurred that night would spread quickly, far more quickly than any good news ever could, in the way that could only happen in a small village. It would likely go before me, instantly changing any sort of reputation that I'd established for myself. My business would likely be ruined, and I realized that most people would shun me until my name had been cleared without question.

There would only be a few people who might be able to help me...

And so I would go to them and ask for the help I so desperately needed.

Irene answered the door when I knocked. Night had fallen, and the darkness filled the sky above us, the stars peeking out from behind the clouds as they lazily danced across the velvety sky.

"Helen," she said, smiling and looking simultaneously

surprised as she pulled the door open. "I'm surprised to see you so late. Is everything all right?"

"No," I said, pushing past her inside the house in the narrow gap she'd left between herself and the door. "No, it's not all right."

When I stepped fully into the light, I heard her gasp behind me. "Helen, what on earth happened – "

"I promise that I will explain everything to you," I said. "But may I please use your shower? And perhaps borrow a change of clothes?"

"Of – of course," Irene said, eyeing the bloody spatters on my clothing and face. "Right this way."

We walked up to her stairs, soon after making our way up to the flat above the teahouse.

Nathanial was sitting at the table, reading the paper. The radio sounded into the room from its place beside the fireplace, Michael sitting before it enraptured as James Barrows' familiar voice told his weekly story of mystery and intrigue, a favorite for many young children in Brookminster.

On seeing me, Nathaniel got to his feet and said, "What on earth – "

"Shh," Irene urged, pressing her finger to her lips. She glanced obviously over to their son, who hadn't noticed our entry into the room. She shook her head and urged me toward the door to the washroom.

"Here you are," she said, turning the shower on, filling the room quickly with hot, wet air. "And of course, you'll need a towel." Opening the linen closet, she procured a pair of fluffy, white towels, setting them down on the side of the sink. "You'll find soap in there, I hope it's the sort that you like."

If only she knew how much I despised the very skin I was in right at that moment; preference for soap was the furthest thing from my mind. "Thank you," I said. "I do appreciate it."

Irene searched my face, and for a moment, I was certain she was going to start asking questions while we had the sound of the running water to mask our voices. She did not, however, and instead turned her back, pulling the door open. "If you need anything, just ask, all right? I'll bring you some clean clothes to change into."

"Thank you," was all I could think to say.

She departed, shutting the door and trapping the heat and steam inside with me.

I peeled the clothes from my body, the dried blood making me gag as it stuck to the hem of my blouse, to the edges of my sleeves, and to the side of the neckline. I managed to discard all my things and tossed them into the bathroom sink. I didn't waste any time turning on the tap, drenching them all the way through. I picked up the bar of soap and began to attack the fabric with it.

Coppery water filled the sink and raced down the drain.

I knew it would take some time to get the blood out, if I would even be able to, in the end.

I climbed into the shower a few moments later, the heat striking me like an iron. I winced as it scorched my skin, turning the flesh on my arms and chest pink, but soon relished the water's ability to wash the blood from my hands and face.

I scrubbed at my hair three different times until I was certain any residue of the blood might be gone. I took to my skin with the soap bar with such force that it left my skin raw and tender, though without a trace of blood to be found.

I nearly ripped off my fingernails attempting to coax the dark, tarry substance out from beneath, though it was reluctant.

Irene came in a while later, insisting that everything was all right and that she'd found something for me to wear. She didn't linger long, either, and I soon heard the soft *click* of the door as she closed it behind her.

I stood there in the shower for a long time, focusing on the way the water felt running through the ends of my hair, down my neck, and watching as it splashed against the bottom of the shower. It mesmerized me, very nearly wiped the terrible events of the night from my mind.

Soon, though, far too soon, the water began to run cold. Either that, or my skin simply had grown used to it. Nevertheless, I realized I couldn't very well stay in there forever, and instead chose to step out and towel off.

I tugged on the sweater Irene had lent me, something too long in the sleeves and long in the waist, in a pleasant powder blue. I matched it with a comfortable pair of trousers that were a bit loose around my waist, but with my belt –

I looked around for my own clothing, and couldn't find it.

I checked inside the closet, wondering if in my uncomfortable stupor I'd somehow decided that shoving my sopping wet clothes inside was a good idea. I found nothing.

I checked behind the doorway, wondering if my things had slipped out of the sink somehow. I couldn't find them there, either.

Panic flooded my veins, turning my face bright red. What did this mean? How could I have lost my clothing like that?

I decided it was best to finish drying myself off and getting dressed, and then ask Irene if she'd seen them in the sink when she came in to leave me the new, clean clothes.

I wrung as much of the water from my dark hair as I could, doing everything I could to avoid eye contact with myself in the small corner of the mirror that the fog had cleared away from. I knew I'd washed the blood away, and had worked the soap into such a lather that it left my skin raw and tender, but I still felt its ghost on my arms, on my face, on my neck...

And Mr. James' face...I couldn't wipe it from my mind. The pain in his eyes, the strain in his voice...

The hardest thing to realize was that I knew I would never hear that voice again.

Thoroughly sober minded, I opened the door to the bathroom, and padded barefoot out into the kitchen.

Irene and Nathanial were both standing in the kitchen. Irene was pouring tea into some fresh cups, while Nathanial stood against the cabinets, his arms crossed.

Irene glanced over at me as I entered. "Just keep your voice down," she said in a low tone. "We just put Michael to bed."

I nodded, wrapping my arms around myself. "Thank you for the clothes," I said. "Did you happen to see where my – "

"Already taken care of, dear," Irene said. "Washing them as we speak."

My face turned scarlet. "Irene, you don't have to do that. They're filthy, and with all the blood – "

"Whose blood is it?" Nathanial asked, her eyes narrow. "I can see that you seem to be all right."

I glanced back and forth between the two of them. "It...it was Mr. James," I said. "I arrived home early this morning from the train back from London, and ended up sleeping most of the day. When I woke, I was starving, and was on my way down to the inn for a meal..."

"You know you could have stopped here," Irene said, her brow falling. "We would have been happy to feed you."

I felt guilt and affection toward her simultaneously. "Perhaps it would have saved me from the night I had tonight..." I said.

"Here, dear, have some tea and sit down," Irene said, pulling back one of the chairs at the kitchen table. "Why don't you tell us what happened?"

I took the seat she offered, sinking rather heavily down into the chair. "As I said, I was on the way to the inn, when I heard someone calling for help..."

I told them everything just as it happened, the same way I told Sam Graves. I left nothing out, even though I knew that telling them everything I'd been feeling and had experienced wouldn't necessarily change anyone's mind about my involvement in the matter. It helped to see the sorrow on Irene and Nathanial's faces as I spoke, and gave me more peace of mind than I'd been able to give myself.

"Mr. James..." Irene said as I wrapped up my story. She leaned back in her chair, her hand clasped over her heart. "How tragic..."

"Yes," Nathanial said, hunched forward on his elbows, his fingers knotted together, partially obscuring his face. "What surprises me most is how quickly Mr. Hodgins jumped to thinking you were the one to do it."

"That's what surprised me as well," Irene said. "Helen, you poor thing...what a terrible night you have had to endure. Not only trying to help Mr. James, but then facing accusations from those people? By the police?..." She shook her head. "Well, knowing how the people of Brookminster operate, I am certain news of what occurred earlier has already spread. There are likely few in the village who don't already know what happened."

"That's what I thought as well," I said, rubbing the sides of my face. "I think it would be best for me to keep the store closed for the next few days while Inspector Graves investigates, hopefully finding the culprit – "

"You'll stay with us," Irene said, her brow furrowing.

"What?" Nathanial and I both said at the same time.

She nodded firmly. "You'll stay with us. Do you have any idea what people might do to you if you were home alone? Harassment would be a weak word to describe it. Not only will people treat you like a criminal until the real one is found, but some might go so far as to damage your property, your home..." She looked over at her husband. "You know that I am right, Nathanial. People will be ruthless, even if she is found to be innocent."

He sighed. "They certainly will be. And from the sounds of it, some in the village are already suspicious of you, Helen. The best way to keep you safe is likely to pretend that you aren't home. Perhaps we could start a rumor that you went out of town to visit family."

I shook my head. "Inspector Graves told me I wasn't allowed to set foot outside of Brookminster."

"Well, of course, but the ordinary people of the village won't know that," Irene said. "It's settled, then. We will put you up in our guest room until this whole thing blows over, yes?"

Nathanial nodded. "I agree. I think it would be best."

5

The next week was one of the worst I'd ever experienced.

Irene had been right. Everyone was out for blood it seemed. My blood. Without evidence, and by word of mouth only, they assumed that I had, in fact, been the one to kill Mr. James.

Irene wouldn't let me work in the teahouse, even though I wanted to do something to help out. She thought it best to keep up the fiction that I had gone away. I did, however, overhear a conversation that she and Nathanial were having the third night I was staying with them.

"Many people are utterly convinced that she is the one who did it," Irene said with exasperation. "They say she may as well be a stranger, having moved to Brookminster so recently."

"Irene, hardly anyone around here knows her like we do," Nathanial said in a reassuring tone. "In their mind, they want justice for a prominent figure in our town. Mr. James's death is going to be felt a lot more deeply than that of a beggar, or a crotchety old woman that no one liked. He was one of the most prestigious people to ever live here. He loved everyone in this town, and was an example of his profession; compassionate, caring, and selfless. His loss will be felt, and deeply."

"I know you're right," Irene said. "But that doesn't mean that Helen is to blame."

"No, it certainly does not," Nathanial said. "But to everyone else, she was the one who had his blood on her hands."

I asked Irene the following morning if I could go out and fetch her groceries for her, but she shrieked at me. "No!" she cried. "No," she said, a little more calmly, smiling. "We have everything we need for now. Besides, I'm not certain you would like to hear what – "

"What everyone in the village has to say, yes I know..." I said.

Later that night, Nathanial informed me that someone had thrown a brick through one of my windows.

My first instinct was to think to ask Sidney to help me repair it...and then with a curdling knot in my stomach, I realized all over again that Sidney had betrayed me, attempted to kill me...and I ended up taking his life in the end. I cried at the dinner table, which seemed to confuse poor Michael, requiring Irene to whisk me away from the table and sit with me in my room while I attempted to pull myself together.

It wasn't until the fifth day staying with the Driscolls that I realized I needed to really concentrate on finding the true killer.

"I can't live like this," I said to Irene as we were having afternoon tea.

Michael was playing out in the yard, the muddy puddles left after the morning rain presenting themselves as a perfect playground for the young lad. He seemed entirely content, which left Irene and I a chance to talk after the teahouse closed up for the day.

"What do you mean?" Irene asked.

"I can't keep living like I am guilty," I said. "I would greatly like to go back to my own home, get some clean clothing, and just be able to walk outside. I haven't left this house in five days…"

Irene's face fell. "I am sorry, dear. I wish there was something more I could do. It's just…I've heard how the people in the village are taking it. Unfortunately, nothing else remotely interesting has happened this week, and it seems to be all anyone can talk about…"

I glared at a knot in the wooden table. "I'm going to miss the funeral, at this rate," I said.

"You won't unless the autopsy is finished rather quickly," she said. "And from what I've heard, the police weren't able to discern anything from it so far."

I shook my head, my hands grasping the teacup. "I need to find who did this," I said. "It might be the only way to clear my name."

"Sam didn't have any other leads?" Irene asked.

I shook my head again. "No," I said. "Not that first night, at least. And he hasn't called to let me know of any. Unless he doesn't know that I've been staying here – "

"I let him know," Irene said. "I thought it might be better than you telling him."

I clamped my mouth shut after that.

"When Mr. James was…well, when he was still conscious…" Irene said. "Didn't it seem like he was trying to tell you who had killed him? Perhaps we can try to discern it from that."

I shook my head. "It was...cryptic, at best. I can't even be sure he wasn't hallucinating, or out of his mind."

"Perhaps," Irene said. "Regardless, what did he say, exactly? Can you remember?"

I pursed my lips, thinking. "Well, it was definitely a 'he'," I said. "And it seemed like he was angry at Mr. James."

"So there was a falling out of some sort before he died," Irene said, frowning at the table. "Hmm...I wonder..."

"What?" I asked. "Do you know something?"

"There's certainly no way to be certain, but there has been a rumor going around town for some time about Mr. James' youngest daughter, Rachel. She walked away from her father's faith when she was younger, running away with someone to London, only to come back six months later with her heart broken."

"That's interesting," I said, my brow furrowing. "I had no idea he had any children."

"They're all grown by now," Irene said. "He and his wife had three children, I believe. Their oldest daughter, Rebecca, is happily married with some children of her own, living in Tuffley, south of Gloucester. I have seen them in church every few weeks, when they come to visit. Their middle, a son named Daniel, lives in the village here as well, though he has been in Oxford studying at the seminary to follow in his father's footsteps. I wonder if he will be the one to take his father's place at the church here in the village..."

"And the youngest daughter?" I asked. "Rachel, you said?"

"Yes," Irene said. "She is quite the handful, from what I've heard. She can't be older than twenty-five, perhaps twenty-six by now. Last I heard, she had taken a fancy to a mechanic here in town, but her parents did not approve of the relationship."

My eyes widened. "Who might this mechanic be?" I asked. "Do you think this might be the sort of lead I should follow up on?"

Irene pursed her lips for a moment. "To be honest, starting with the James family may not be the worst idea..." she said. "Though you might have a difficult time speaking with them if they know who you are, and that you are being investigated for the murder of their father..."

"What about this mechanic, though?" I asked. "He likely wouldn't know me, especially if things never went anywhere between him and Rachel."

Irene slowly nodded her head. "I imagine he wouldn't be paying as close attention to the whole ordeal as Rachel would be."

"Then maybe I should go and see him," I said. "If he does anything the least bit suspicious, I could – "

"Who is doing something suspicious?"

Nathanial had wandered into the kitchen. He glanced back and forth between Irene and me, his face scrutinizing.

"We think we may have found a suspect," I said. "At least, right now it's the best lead I have."

"I see," Nathanial said, walking past us to the ice box.

"Do you know anything about the mechanic that Mr. James' daughter was interested in?" I asked Nathanial. "What is his name, Irene?"

"Oh, I'm not certain of his name," Irene said, her face turning pink. She had averted her eyes, and seemed far more interested in the tabletop suddenly than her husband who she usually beamed at whenever he walked into the room.

Nathanial, too, suddenly seemed rather cool, his eyes glued to the side of the ice box that he had just pulled some milk from.

I stared at Nathanial for a long moment, hoping he might answer me.

"I don't know," he said, an edge to his words. He pulled open the ice box and deposited the milk back inside, not bothering to drink any of it. "Aren't you wasting your time, chasing rumors?"

I glared at him. "What else do I have to go on?"

He wouldn't look me in the eye, and didn't seem to have an answer to my question.

A nasty suspicion rose up within me, making my ears warm. "You...you actually think I did it...don't you, Nathanial?"

That made him look at me. In that moment, I saw something that I never really expected to ever see.

Doubt.

"No," he said a second too late. "I don't think you – "

"Yes you do," I said, slowly getting to my feet. "You think that I killed Mr. James."

"Helen, please," Irene said. "He certainly does not believe that. Nathanial, you don't believe that."

"I already said I didn't," he said. "I thought I made that clear."

"You hesitated," I said, my eyes narrowing.

"How can you expect me to answer that sort of weighted question so quickly?" he asked, his voice beginning to rise.

"Easily, I think," I said, my own voice rising to match his. "I didn't realize that you thought so little of me – "

"Helen," Irene said in an icy tone. "You should watch the level of your voice. Both of you should."

I wheeled around and looked at her, my heart hammering against my ribs. "And what about you?" I asked. "Do you think I killed him, too?"

"Absolutely not," Irene said, her brow furrowing together. "How could you ask such a thing?"

"Your husband seems to doubt me enough," I said.

"I already said I didn't – " Nathanial said.

"You didn't have to," I said, turning and glaring at him. "Your expression said everything that you weren't brave enough to say."

"Helen, really," Irene snapped. "I understand you're upset about all this, but taking it out on us is just – "

"You are completely missing Nathanial's response," I said, gesturing over to him. I turned and glared at him again. "Who did you speak with? Mr. Hodgins? Did his account seem more believable than mine, someone who only just got here a few months ago?"

Nathanial's eyes widened. "You...overheard that?"

"That was our private conversation," Irene snapped, going to stand beside her husband. "I'm surprised at you, Helen. Do you not trust us?"

"I'm..." I started, looking back and forth between the two of them.

I didn't have anything else to say, so I turned on my heel and stomped off toward the guest room, my ears ringing as I went.

I slammed the door behind me, not even caring about the sound that must have echoed all the way through the house. As soon as I slumped against the wooden frame, I burst into tears, sliding down the wall, all the way to the floor.

My life was falling apart around me, and there was nothing I could do to set things right. All I could do was wallow in my own self pity, taking solace in the four walls of the small room I called my own.

6

The knots in my stomach never did leave me for the rest of the night. Nor would my mind rest long enough to allow me to sleep. I tossed and turned, unable to reconcile myself to what had happened with Nathanial and Irene.

I couldn't bring myself to get up and apologize to them in person. For some reason, my pride insisted that they should be the ones to apologize to me for the way they had so terribly treated me...especially Nathanial. How could he think that I had killed Mr. James? What had I done since meeting him that would make him question my honesty and integrity, even for a moment?

I heard them retire to bed around ten that evening, and still all I could do was lay there and stare up at the ceiling. Everything felt wrong inside of me. There was no peace for my heart, and already struggling with the fear and sorrow of Mr. James' death, I found myself piling on the guilt now with Irene and Nathanial.

In the end, around two in the morning, I had to admit to myself that I was the one in the wrong.

Nathanial only has my word to go off of, I thought bitterly and reluctantly. *Given the fact I showed up at their house almost a week ago now covered in a dead man's blood, I need to give him the benefit of the doubt that something incredibly strange must be happening here.*

I wondered what Roger would think if he knew about this whole situation. Given my suspicions that he was the one following me, watching me from the shadows, I wondered if he already knew the rumors going around...and whether or not he believed them in the first place.

I finally dragged myself out of bed just before five in the morning, knowing that sleep was just not going to come. I needed to make things right, and I realized there was really only one way to do so.

I slowly made my way down to the teashop, careful not to disturb the household. I set my suitcase, all packed up, down beside the hostess table. There I found a pad of paper that Irene used to mark down seating order for guests, along with a few pens. Plucking one from the table, I tore a piece of paper from the pad and wandered over to the nearest table, sitting down.

In the dim light spilling in from the street lamp outside, I wrote the letter I'd been forming in my mind since a few hours before.

Dear Irene and Nathanial,

First of all, I want to apologize for my behavior last night. I let my anger at the whole situation get the better of me, and must admit to feeling a bit like a rabbit caught in a trap. This ordeal has me frightened, and while I know there are many in the village who don't believe I am innocent, to hear a dear friend hesitate was a shock.

I am sorry for getting as upset as I did, and for acting out in your home that way. You both have been so kind to me, offering me sanctuary during this difficult time in my life. I am undeserving of your hospitality, and realize that by my actions last night, I have negated my ability to stay with you any longer. I would not feel right imposing on you any further, especially given the situation I put us all into last night.

I will not cause you any more harm, and will instead try to find out who this person was that so thoughtlessly took Mr. James' life.

Thank you for all your love and care, and for opening your home to me, despite all of the accusations. I am truly grateful.

With all my love,

Helen Lightholder

I read it over a few times to make sure that my exhausted mind had written something relatively coherent. Pleased that it seemed to be clear, I folded it up and set it beside the till in the back, where I knew Irene would see it as she prepared to open the teahouse for the day.

With a heavy sigh, I picked up my suitcase and headed for the door, determined not to make a sound that would draw their attention from upstairs.

It had been six days since I'd been outside on High Street. Granted, the last time I'd been out there, I had left the police station, covered in blood, wondering how in the world I was going to make it through the rest of the day.

While my circumstances had hardly changed since then, I found my anger as good a source for my determination as anything else I had felt up to that point.

I had one goal in mind, and that was hopefully going to

be easy enough to meet. I needed to find the mechanic that Irene had mentioned, and see if he knew anything about Mr. James...or tried to deny knowing him in the first place.

That was what pushed me to be able to open the front door of my cottage, to be able to stare at the broken window with some semblance of sanity, and be able step inside without caring whether or not someone was going to come to call and complain or make trouble for me.

I knew that going out in public was going to do nothing for me. If anything, people would refuse to help me, given the fact that I was the lead suspect for the case in the first place.

So I decided to attempt the next best thing, and make some calls around the village.

Sidney hadn't left me entirely without knowledge. Whether or not he had known it at the time, some of his tricks had passed to me. His accent, for example. I never teased him about it much, but I always liked the sound of it. And learning that he was not, in fact, Scottish in the end, it helped me to realize that I, too, could probably learn how to use an accent to some successful degree.

I picked up the phone and dialed the first number I could think of that wasn't Irene.

Mrs. Georgianna.

The phone rang a few times, but being elderly like she was, I knew that she must have already been awake, milling about her house, likely readying herself for some social event she would probably be attending that evening.

"Hello?" she asked finally when she answered the phone.

"Yes, hello, is this Mrs. Georgianna?" I asked, attempting

my best Scottish accent. It was rather poor, but I did my best to say the words in the same way Sidney would have.

"Yes, it is, but who is this?" she asked. "I don't recognize your voice."

"We haven't met yet," I said. "I'm Gwen's cousin. From the north?"

"Gwen?" Mrs. Georgianna said. "Gwen who?"

My face flushed. I had been hoping that she would just accept any name and go along with it, perhaps out of politeness. Maybe she still would. "Gwen Thomas. Oh come now, you are all she speaks about. She says you have such exquisite taste, and are always the talk of all the parties in the village..."

"Oh, well, yes, I suppose I am," Mrs. Georgianna said with a little chuckle.

It seemed that Sidney was right about another thing; a little flattery went a long way.

"Well, what can I do for you, Miss...?"

"Miss Thomas as well, ma'am. Francine Thomas. Well, my dear cousin instructed me to call you, insisting that you would surely be the best one to help me with my problem," I said. I felt my accent slipping a few times as I tried to rush through the words, and had to force myself to slow down so as to not upset the charade.

I heard another laugh on the line. "I can certainly try to help you, dear. What is it that you need?"

"This might sound strange, you know, but I am in great need of a mechanic," I said. "A good one, mind you. It's my husband's car, you see. He's away, and sometimes I think he loves that car more than he loves me. Anyway, I promised him that I would get it serviced every three months while he was away, and wouldn't you know that the time for the servicing has arrived while I am staying with my cousin?"

"Oh, yes, men can certainly be particular about their vehicles," Mrs. Georgianna said. "My late husband was quite a motor enthusiast himself. He loved to go out for Saturday drives, eager to show off his pride and joy to anyone he might pass by..." There was a happy sigh on the other end.

I was pleased to see that the knowledge I'd learned about her over the years had finally paid off. A talkative woman, she would often keep me well occupied when she would come into the haberdashery, and talk for so long and so often that I would have to excuse myself to help disgruntled customers who felt they were being ignored.

"My cousin was right, you certainly were the right woman to call," I said. "Do you by any chance know of a younger man who might be able to get the job done sooner rather than later? I do have a tight schedule to keep."

"Oh, I certainly do, yes," Mrs. Georgianna said. "You might try Lucas Adams. Quite the young fellow, and I heard that he was rather sweet on the daughter of that poor minister who just passed away."

She couldn't have made that any easier.

After saying goodbye, I felt simultaneously pleased with myself for being able to hold an accent as long as I had, as well as happy with my quick thinking and ingenuity at retrieving the information I needed. The old lady was bound to be confused later when she realized that she did not, in fact, know a Gwen Thomas, but I hoped she would remain ignorant of the fact until the investigation was over and done with.

Was it lying? Certainly. Would it harm Mrs. Georgianna in any way? Not in any way that I could see, no.

Lucas Adams was a name I had heard around the village before. Mr. Diggory had mentioned him once before, and I was certain Sidney had worked with him on more than one occasion. That made sense, given the fact that the two men must have been about the same age.

After a quick look through the telephone book, I managed to locate the address of Lucas' shop, and saw it opened right at eight. I wasted no time having a shower, changing my clothes into something that might conceal my identity more than usual, and setting out into the bright morning sunshine.

I pulled the hat I'd thrown on low over my face as I walked. I'd chosen something I would have worn back in Plymouth, something that was much less flashy than I normally would wear, hoping it would keep people's attention away from me. A drab dress of beige and cream, I knew that it was something Roger would have asked me to get rid of before long. It hung over my shoulders, much like a tent.

The mechanic's shop was down High Street, and then left onto Rose Avenue, and then down on the corner of Walsingham and Themes Roads.

It was a small shop that seemed to be in the middle of more projects than it could possibly handle. Over a dozen cars sat out in the front drive, some of which were missing doors, another of which was missing all four of its tires. A lovely red car had the bonnet pulled up, and the engine inside seemed to be in pieces.

The garage itself was tucked back against a tree line that seemed to follow the river that circled the village. The doors to the garage had been thrown open already, and a catchy jazz number filtered out into the morning air.

I approached the office door alongside the garage, and

struggled to push it open as it seemed to be still locked. I pushed my weight against it, the knob turning, but the door itself seemed to be –

"Jammed," said a voice behind me. "It does that in the early mornings sometimes. Just give it a good shove."

I glanced over my shoulder and saw a young man who couldn't have been much older than I was. He looked like what I'd imagined a mechanic would, with grease stained fingertips, ratty clothing and a sleeveless shirt that revealed lean but well-toned arm muscles, and an oil rag hanging out of his pocket. There was a smudge of some sort of oily fluid across his cheekbone, and sweat beaded up along his dark hairline. A rather scruffy beard covered most of his jaw, but it did nothing to hide his young face.

"Oh, thank you," I said, but I turned away from the door. "Do you by any chance know where I might be able to find Lucas Adams?"

The man's green eyes narrowed. "And who might be asking?" he asked, pulling the rag from his pocket and wiping his hands on it.

"I don't mean to be nosey, but I...well, I'm trying to help reach out to those who knew Mr. James and his family, and I – "

"I've got nothing to say to you..." Lucas said darkly, his face screwing up as he brushed past me to the door. With one good shove with his arm, he managed to unstick it, and strode inside.

I hesitated for only a brief moment before following after.

"Mr. Adams, I am simply reaching out to those who might have been affected by his death, and know that you had connections to the family when – "

He rounded on me, not bothering to hide the anger in his gaze. "I don't know who told you what, but my connection with his family is long since passed," he said in a low rumble. "Now if you would kindly tell me what it is about your vehicle I can help you with, then I can certainly take care of you."

I was well aware of the danger in his voice, and not wanting to step on any toes, I held up my hands defensively. "I do not wish to trouble you, Mr. Adams," I said in as gentle of a voice as I could muster. "My only hope was to offer you some help if it was needed – "

"I don't need any help," he said. "I've made my peace with it. Mr. James was..." his voice trailed off just as my ears perked up. "It's sad what happened to him, but I have kept my distance on purpose. Now please. If you don't need anything else, I must get back to work."

He disappeared behind another door, labeled with an *Employees Only* sign.

I bit down on my lip, looking around.

The shop itself was quiet. Whoever the cars that he had been working on belonged to, they clearly were not here at the moment.

I wondered if Lucas was the only one here, or if there were other mechanics who worked at the shop. To check, I made my way to the garage, peering outside.

There didn't seem to be any sound apart from the radio playing yet another jazz piece. Everything was still, including the cars that were lifted up high above my head on motorized platforms.

I paused. Would there be anything in here that might point me to whether or not Lucas Adams was the killer I was looking for? Or would I have to look elsewhere?

I glanced over my shoulder, back into the shop, where my eyes fell on the door that Lucas had walked into.

That is likely where he would keep his personal belongings. There, and in an office.

I wandered back out to the front of the shop, hoping to catch a glimpse of Lucas heading back out to the shop, leaving me with an opening to sneak in and look around while he was busy with a car or another customer.

I leaned against the wall, listening as hard as I could.

It was clear that Lucas knew exactly what I was talking about. The flash in his eyes had made my stomach flip over, and it made me sure that he was the one I had been looking for.

Was his desire to avoid talking about Mr. James because of his involvement in his murder? Or had his relationship with the vicar's daughter gone badly?

I was not going to get any more information out of Lucas, that much was obvious.

Searching his office or through his personal belongings seemed like the best place to start.

I only had to wait another quarter of an hour before Lucas made his way back out into the garage, whistling through his teeth. I heard the clank of a metal tool against the frame of one of the cars. The music soon grew in volume, and he began to sing along.

Knowing that my time had come, I snuck back to the door to the shop. Glancing over my shoulder to make sure he hadn't wandered back out into the front drive, I casually leaned against the door as if I was meant to be there, and stepped inside with confidence.

The music was faint through the walls of the inner shop, but I could also still make out his singing.

I made my way to the door, waiting just a moment before slipping inside, latching the door behind me.

It was a small room, with an overcrowded desk, a cluttered shelf, and an old, torn up leather chair. A stack of clothes sat on an old, worn armchair along the wall, a mixture of ordinary clothes and work clothes. The room smelled heavily of axel grease, gasoline, and burnt rubber.

*This is going to take forever to go through...*I thought.

I walked around the desk, looking at the stacks of papers that were balanced precariously on top. I feared that if I sneezed, they might go flying, and I knew I would never be able to put them all back the way they were.

I imagined that if Roger were to instruct me on the best way to investigate a place, his advice would be to leave it just as I found it so as to not tip off the person I was investigating that I was onto them.

I pulled the top drawer of the desk open, but found nothing more than a hodgepodge of pens, loose notes, and order forms. There was nothing to indicate that Lucas was anything other than a hard worker. Even as I looked up and around the room, I realized there wasn't a shred of personal information in the room. Not a photo, not a list of what to pick up at the grocery store.

That's strange, isn't it? I realized. *If this is where he works, all day, every day, wouldn't he want something here to remind him that work isn't his entire life? Unless...work* is *his entire life.*

That was an interesting premise. Would I have to go and search his home instead? That would surely be a feat to find. I could always follow him home...

I stepped around the far side of the desk, and gasped as my foot caught something rather heavy and bulky, nearly causing me to trip over myself.

I looked down and saw a pair of boots beside the desk. Thick soled and made of leather, the boots appeared to be as well worn as the chair behind the desk. They were also covered in a dried mud that had flaked off and scattered on the floor beneath it.

Typically, I wouldn't have thought twice about dirty boots in the middle of a dirty office...but something about the color of the mud caught my attention.

It had a great deal of clay in it, much like the dirt along the river...but there was one other place that I had seen it.

A detail I would have likely overlooked had I not recently been standing at the side of a grave when it was being dug...or even more recently watching the life leave a man who was dying, his fingers caked in the muddy dirt...

The church cemetery. The dirt at the churchyard had the same reddish clay mixed within it.

This is quite a stretch, though, I thought. *The river right behind the shop here might very well have the same sort of dirt along the bank. I cannot be sure that the dirt on the boots is the same as that from the cemetery.*

Even still...the boots were hidden, weren't they? Tucked away, out of sight. And who else would come in here but Lucas in the first place?

I chewed on the inside of my lip, wondering if this was enough to call Sam and let him know what I'd found. He was going to have to have a good reason to barge into this office to check it. And even if he could, then would Lucas simply lie about it all in the first place? Would it end in a dead end after all that trouble?

I quickly made my way out of the office after one final look around, coming up empty apart from the boots.

It was certainly weak evidence, but it was the first step

I'd taken toward finding the real killer of Mr. James, and gave me more hope than I'd felt in days. I would find the person who had taken his life so carelessly, and I would certainly find a way to clear my own name so that I could go back to living in this village.

I made my way outside, and started down the road, worrying that Lucas might have seen me leave. I wished he would have spoken to me, but at least I knew that Sam would certainly be interested in hearing about the man who had been denied the chance to see Mr. James' daughter. That alone might be enough to open up the case once again and consider more suspects.

I allowed myself one smile of relief. Just one. A life had still been lost, and my reputation was still on the line. This was far from over.

But that didn't mean that a resolution wasn't worth fighting toward.

7

I made my way from the autobody shop as quickly, yet as casually as I could. I didn't want to be seen hurrying away. If anyone were to notice me, then I knew that too many questions would be asked...not to mention the accusations about what on earth I was doing all dressed up in a disguise and snooping around a place like that.

I realized my trip might very well have been in vain. Lucas Adams may or may not have been the killer, and I was no closer to discovering the truth.

Was his reaction more out of heartbreak? Or guilt? That was the question I kept rolling around in my mind as I stepped back onto High Street, which was starting to wake up, becoming a great deal busier and livelier. Women strung clothes from their lines in their back gardens to hang in the sunshine, while Mr. Webster delivered the post from the back of his bicycle. Mrs. William's dog chased her son down the street, while the boy pulled a kite after him, laughing as the wind caught the sail, lifting it high into the sky.

Brookminster, for all the sinister happenings in its underbelly, really was a charming little village, filled with good people with good intentions. It broke my heart to see that darkness could exist in such a warm, welcoming place.

More and more, I was beginning to understand Sam Graves' outlook on the world. Being jaded was not something I ever wanted, but that didn't mean that the world around me wasn't going to push and shove me in that direction, in the end.

It made me wonder how Roger really saw things. These were the sorts of things we never spoke about, him and I. Of course we talked of the world at large, what it would be like, hopefully, when the war was over. We dreamt of what our lives would look like, the places we could travel to safely once again, the years of joy we would have with one another.

My heart skipped. For so long, I had been so utterly convinced, with good reason, that those dreams would never come to fruition, that he was dead and gone, and that I would never see him again.

Until that day, in the alleyway…

It was him. I was sure of it.

As it had before, my heart began to stir with these new realizations about what my life *could* be like now. There had been no indication that Roger wanted any further contact with me, apart from his appearance now and again in the shadows, watching me. Even if he had been told to end any and all contact with those he had known, he had still given me the chance to know that it was him. Why? Why hadn't he spoken? Why had he allowed me to see him? Didn't he realize this brought up so many new questions that I was desperate to ask him?

Perhaps he wanted me to be patient, or to work out the answers on my own. He had kept his distance enough to let me discern the truth of what was happening in Brookminster alone. He had done nothing to interfere, or to help in any way. I couldn't help but feel mingled frustration and admiration in that. He either trusted me enough to do these things on my own, or he had little care for what happened to me now.

Was it possible that I was nothing more than a means to an end for him? Could all of his honeyed words and his sweet nothings have been hollow?

No. That wasn't Roger. He really did love me once. Whether or not that was still true was a question I could not answer. Not yet, at least.

As I made my way along High Street, I kept my hat pulled low over my face, the sunglasses I wore obscuring my eyes, and the scarf around my neck protecting what little of my face remained exposed as it flowed in the wind.

I kept my eyes on the road ahead of me, determined to make it home so I could call Inspector Graves and ask him about what my next steps should be, and whether or not he saw value in what I had discovered in Lucas Adams' office.

Something up ahead seemed...off to me. While all the others in the village were moving about, hurrying on their ways while the sun still shone in the summer sky, there was one figure that stood entirely still, almost as if he were invisible to the rest of the townsfolk. They walked around his broad-shouldered stature as if he were nothing more than a tree, not even sparing a glance for him.

His face, too, was obscured by a rather handsome fedora, the shadows preventing me from seeing his features clearly.

His shoulders were relaxed, and his hands were slid into the pockets of his trench coat.

One thing was for certain, though. His eyes were fixed upon me.

I stopped, staring at the figure, my heart skipping in my chest.

"Roger...?" I mouthed to him, shock coursing through me, surprise that he would let me see him for this long, let others in the street see him, as well.

He didn't acknowledge my question, instead turning toward the alleyway between the inn and the flower shop.

It was clear he wanted me to follow him.

I did just that, and did not dawdle.

I didn't, at the same time, want to make it too obvious that I was following. I wanted to be sure that we weren't going to be trailed by anyone, in case this was the first time we got to speak with one another.

My heart was pounding as I rounded the corner, the shadow of the elm tree growing between the two shops cool and inviting.

I went to pull the hat off my head so I could see him more clearly...when I realized that the alleyway was empty once again.

He had managed to escape without me noticing.

I frowned into the shadowed alley, wondering how he could have possibly done that again. It seemed like every time I got close to him, he managed to find a way to keep his distance.

I opened my mouth to say something, but closed it shortly after. If some other unseen person was listening in, I didn't want to give Roger or his position away. One thing was for certain; he wanted me to know he was there, and that he was watching.

It was somewhat reassuring to realize that he was watching after me. Much like a guardian angel, he kept close tabs on me and ensured that I was doing all right.

It made me wonder...had he been watching me as I went and inspected Lucas Adams' shop? Had he followed me all the way there?

And why had he chosen now to reveal himself again? Was it meant to be a message? Was he trying to communicate with me?

I looked over my shoulder; no one had followed me into the alleyway. And looking further into the alley, all the way to the other side where sunlight spilled in between the homes, there was no one.

But Roger couldn't have gotten far. That much I knew for certain.

I wished I could leave him a letter somewhere where he could easily find it. I supposed I could leave one in the postbox in front of my house, but it might seem strange if someone were to see him taking a letter from there as opposed to leaving one.

How would a spy communicate? Letters could be intercepted. Roger knew this, which was why the code he'd hidden in the letter to me had been so obscure, so muted that anyone who wasn't a spy would have thought nothing of it.

Perhaps a letter was not the best way. Then how?

It wasn't as if I had much to leave behind to let him know that I had recognized him. My wedding ring was back at home, tucked away inside my jewelry box, and I didn't feel comfortable just leaving that out somewhere for someone else to find.

I touched my hat, considering the ribbon I'd tied around it, but quickly discerned that would likely fly away before Roger was able to get to it.

Something more substantial, but perhaps less valuable?

My hand fell over a brooch keeping the scarf wrapped around my neck. It had once belonged to my mother, though it had been in my possession for some time now. I was certain Roger would recognize it, as I'd worn it once or twice when he'd taken me dancing.

The jewel encrusted lily was quite special to me, but it would likely be seen as nothing more than a costume piece to someone else, not worth much monetarily.

I undid the brooch, and looked around for a place to keep it safe, where someone else wouldn't happen upon it.

The low rock wall that ran along either side of the narrow pathway in the alleyway must have been as ancient as the one that encircled my own home. And there were likely just as many loose rocks.

It only took me a few moments of testing the stability of the rocks to find a loose enough one. Lifting it, I found a shallow indent in the mortar that was meant to hold the stone in place. I set the brooch down inside it, and covered it once again with the rock.

I smiled. It was entirely inconspicuous now.

But how would Roger know where to find it?

I noticed names carved into the rocks of the walls of the surrounding buildings as well as the paths. Young men and women professing their love for one another, or people leaving behind messages of anger or hate, most of which had been scratched out by other rocks. The main graffiti I saw, though, were initials. Especially initials drawn inside of hearts scratched into the rocks.

I grinned.

Picking up a rock with a jagged edge, I, too, scrawled a heart into the stone that I'd tucked the brooch away underneath, followed by four initials.

R.L. & H.L.

The note fit in well among the others, and would likely go entirely unnoticed...except, I hoped, by Roger.

Content with my own clever thinking, determined to come back and check in a day or two and see if the brooch was still there, I stood to my feet, dusting the powdered rock from my palms. I knew that if anyone else were to pass through here, they would not see the note, and they would never think to check under the rock.

I turned and walked from the alley, feeling quite hopeful that I was about to communicate with the man who I had once considered dead, in a secretive way that only the two of us would know about.

I started toward home when a voice made me stop dead in my tracks.

"I thought that was you, slipping away into the alley..."

I wheeled around and found myself standing face to face with Irene...and she looked none too pleased.

"Irene," I said, pulling the hat lower over my face while simultaneously pushing the sunglasses up the bridge of my nose. "How did you recognize me – "

"What on earth were you doing back there?" she asked in the motherly tone only she could use.

I looked up at her, my cheeks flushing scarlet. "N – nothing," I said automatically, and immediately regretted it. "Just – just stepped out of the sun for a moment."

Irene's brow furrowed, her hands planted firmly on her hips. "Why don't you come with me?" she asked. "I think there are some things that we need to discuss."

A lump formed in my throat, but I didn't argue with her. She was certainly right that there were things that had gone unaddressed between us, which were going to need addressing.

I fell into step behind her, and followed her across the street toward the teahouse, which was just up the road a ways.

I felt a bit like a schoolgirl who had skipped out on class, or been caught sleeping during a lesson. I wasn't sure why the guilt was as strong as it was, but as we neared Irene's house, the argument I'd had with her and Nathanial came back full force in my memory, and I began to wonder if she was simply pulling me aside so that she could scold me again for how I'd acted.

I wouldn't have blamed her, but the truth was I had a great deal more on my mind than I had that morning when I left their house before they'd all woken up.

We walked into the teahouse, which was rather busy for a Friday morning, which was when most people went and stocked up on their goods for the week. Ration tickets were spent, and sometimes there wasn't enough for anything non-essential. Weekends were certainly not what they used to be.

Nevertheless, it seemed everyone was out enjoying the lovely weather, likely thinking it could be one of the last nice summer days before autumn began to settle into the rolling hills, turning the trees from their vibrant, lush green, to the golden and amber hues of the last season before winter.

"Come with me," Irene whispered over her shoulder as we wound our way through the tables, most of which were full by now.

A few of the patrons turned to look up at me as we passed, but I didn't see recognition on any of their faces as we made our way toward the back of the room.

Irene pushed the kitchen door open, striding inside. I followed after, keeping pace.

As soon as the door closed, though, she rounded on me, prodding me in the chest. "Why on earth did you think it was all right to just up and leave this morning like you did?" she asked.

I hesitated, gaping at her. "I – I thought it was best – " I started.

Irene shook her head. "No. It was not best. And take off that ridiculous disguise. I knew it was you the moment I saw you."

Deflated, I slowly removed the hat and the glasses, and untied the scarf from around my neck. I set them all down on the counter before looking back at her.

Like a mother waiting for a confession from her child, she glared at me, her arms folded across her chest.

"What were you doing out there in that alley?" she asked. "And don't say 'nothing'. I saw you as you wandered in there. I have no idea what could have been back there for you, but I'm certain it couldn't have been anything good."

I cleared my throat. "I thought I saw someone," I said, trying to be as honest as I could without giving everything away. "But I think I was mistaken. Sometimes it feels like I'm chasing ghosts lately..."

Irene's stony face relaxed as she let out a heavy sigh, her shoulders sagging. "Helen..." she said. "To be honest, I'm not really sure what to think of you lately. Ever since you came back from London the first time, something has been different about you." Her tone held mingled exasperation and sadness. "And I don't know if it's something we did, or said, that makes you feel like you can't trust us anymore – "

"It's not that I can't trust you," I said at once. "It's not that at all. It's just…"

I didn't really know how to answer her. The truth was, Roger was alive. But that was a truth that I couldn't tell anybody…not even my dearest friend.

"I found out some things in London that…well, it really shocked me," I said. "I came home and found out even more from Sidney when I went and investigated him for Wilson Baxter's murder. Like I told you, he had ties to my husband. This whole thing went far deeper, and far wider than I could ever have imagined…"

"And because of those ties, there are things you cannot tell me, correct?" Irene asked.

I nodded. "It's a government secret. I don't think even I'm supposed to know. That knowledge should have died with me when Sidney had intended to kill me…"

Irene suppressed a shudder. "And even after all this with your late husband, you now have to face persecution for a murder that you did not commit," she said.

Her grey eyes searched mine for a long moment, and I couldn't quite tell what she was thinking. Was she angry? Regretful? Pitying? It was hard to tell.

She sighed eventually, lowering her arms and regarding me with more gentleness.

"Helen…" she said. "I wish you would have stayed this morning. I wish we could have talked things over once everyone had a cooler head. Nathanial and I are not angry with you, not in the least. And I hope you know that he *does* trust you. I think seeing you as distraught and as messy as you were really shook him, and after Sidney's betrayal, I think he was cautious to give his trust so freely again. We had that man in our home so many times...completely unaware that he was not who he said he was..."

"I know," I said, barely above a whisper. "And I'm sorry for bringing him into your life."

"You did nothing of the sort," Irene said firmly. "We fell in love with his character just like everyone in the village did. There is no shame in that. All of the blame rests on him, and his deceit. Please don't go punishing yourself for his actions. They were not your responsibility, regardless of his ties to Roger."

My fingers drummed against my arm as I stared down at the floor. She was right, and I was well aware of it. It didn't help, though, that those were the exact things that passed through my mind most nights as I laid down to go to sleep.

"Look," Irene said. "We may not know everything that is going on with you, but I believe you when you say that you can't tell us some of what's happened. I don't believe that you are holding anything back from us just because you like to be difficult or secretive. I have come to accept this. I know that we can trust you, fully and completely."

My jaw clenched, and my eyes stung. "I don't deserve this sort of kindness," I said. "Especially not after how I treated you and Nathanial last night..."

I heard her footsteps as she walked over to me. She pulled me into a hug, squeezing me tightly. "It's all right," she murmured. "We forgive you for what happened. We love you dearly, and I hope that you know that. We think of you as family, too."

I hugged her back, fighting back the tears that threatened to spill out onto Irene's nice powder blue dress.

She released me, taking a step back. "Now...would you care to tell me why you were walking around town in a disguise like that?"

I sniffed, rubbing at my face. "I think I may have found a lead. You may have been right about that mechanic."

"I'll make a pot of tea," she said while making her way to the stove. "And you can tell me all about it."

As I started to tell her about my telephone call to Mrs. Georgianna that morning, I realized in the back of my mind that I did not deserve Irene's friendship. Her implicit trust in me was both humbling and overwhelming.

I wanted to tell her about Roger. I wanted to tell her everything, so that this fear, this emptiness within me could be shared with someone else.

Even though I knew that Roger was alive...I realized I felt more alone now than I ever had before.

8

A fter I explained everything about Lucas Adams and the boots I'd discovered in his office, Irene insisted that I call Sam Graves.

"It may not be anything, or it could be everything," she said. "He would be the best one to evaluate the information you managed to find."

So I called him. He seemed interested in Lucas, as he had come across his name when he's gone to visit the family of Mr. James in his investigation.

"You always seem to be one step ahead of me," he said with a low chuckle. "I don't know how you do it."

"I thought that would be rather obvious," I said. "I don't have the same restrictions and requirements that you do. It makes finding information a little easier."

He laughed. "Well, very good. I'll check in on him, see if there's anything there. I don't want you to approach him again, though. Now that we're onto a possible lead, it'd be safest for you to keep your distance from that young man."

I didn't argue. Feeling more hopeful now that Irene and

Nathanial were on my side again, and Sam was off to investigate a lead I'd found, I decided to allow myself a chance to relax.

"You're going to stay with us again, right?" Irene asked as I helped her by cleaning the cups she and Nathanial brought back into the kitchen as guests left. "I won't have you in that house all by yourself until this whole matter is dealt with properly."

I didn't want to argue, especially since there were still many people in the village who would consider me to be the culprit in Mr. James' murder. "Very well," I said. "But I really must fetch some clean clothes from my house."

"We will go together as soon as we close up for the day," Irene said.

As we cleaned the tables that afternoon, Irene told Nathanial our plans. He had apologized profusely as soon as he had seen me earlier, telling me how terrible he felt about the way we had left things the night before. We hugged and all was well once again. I was nearly giddy with relief as I did my best to get their dishes as clean as I possibly could.

"I'll go with you, of course," he said. "If someone were to see Helen, I wouldn't want it to just be the two of you having to deal with them. If there's three of us, people will be less likely to provoke you."

I was not going to argue with his logic, especially if someone decided to choose more violent means to show their suspicion of me.

We dropped Michael off at the Diggory's so he could play with their youngest son while the rest of us made our way back down High Street toward my cottage.

"I do appreciate you both, so very much," I said as we walked.

"It's quite all right," Irene said. "You don't have to keep saying that, you know."

"I feel as if I need to make up for how I acted last night," I said.

"You were frightened," Nathanial said. "Anyone with two eyes could have seen that. And for me to be reluctant to give you the support you needed was foolish. I should be the one apologizing."

"But how could you have known that I wasn't like Sidney?" I asked. "Your assumption about that could have been completely correct."

"It's because we trust you, Helen," Nathanial said. "Especially Irene. She knows that you're a good person. I believe her. And I believe you."

Irene smiled, and then as she turned her face, something up ahead made her eyes widen. She reached out her arm, stopping both Nathanial and I in our tracks.

"What is it?" I asked.

Irene's face reflected more horror than surprise.

Part of me didn't want to follow her gaze.

"Let's just go back," she said, attempting to turn me around. "We can always retrieve your clothes another time –"

I pushed her hands aside, though, and searched for what had distressed her so much.

It didn't take long for me to see what it was that had disturbed her.

What amazed me was that I had been home just a few hours before. When I did, everything seemed perfectly ordinary. Yes, the front window was broken, and a layer of dust had settled over all the tables and cabinets inside the shop from nearly a full week of neglect...

However, it had looked nothing like it did now...and I couldn't find the strength to continue standing.

Somehow, it seemed that in the few hours I was gone, some of the villagers had joined forces against me.

Hand-painted signs had been stuck into my front garden, with "*Banish the Killer*" and "*Your guilt will find you out*" among the first I noticed. More signs, also hand written, were tacked to the front of my door with nails that pierced through the fresh coat of blue paint that I'd just given it a few weeks before. I read "*Hypocrite*" and "*Liar*" and "*Murderer*" before even getting to the ones on the second line.

"Come on..." Irene urged me, trying to pull me away from the hatred that seemed to be emanating off the house itself.

I felt sick. How could these people treat me this way? These people who had been kind to me for as long as I had been here in Brookminster. Had it all been a lie? Were they finally showing their true colors?

"This is a disgrace..." Nathanial said in a low growl, stomping over to the garden. He wrenched the gate open and strode up the path, grabbing the signs in the yard, yanking them free from the dirt.

Irene wrapped her arms around my shoulders, while together we watched Nathanial tear the notes down from the door. He wound them up into tight balls, shoving them deep into his pockets.

"Why?" I asked, hopelessly. "Why are they being so cruel?"

"I don't know..." Irene said in a low voice. "But they should be ashamed of themselves. If we knew who did this, we could take their names to the police and let Inspector Graves handle them. This is vandalism!"

Nathanial pulled another sign from the yard free, sending fresh dirt flying against the legs of his trousers. "There aren't any names, unfortunately," he said, looking the sign over from front to back. "I don't recognize the handwriting, either."

"It wasn't here this morning," I said. "None of this was."

"We'll get to the bottom of this," Irene said as Nathanial walked around to the back of the house to check. "Don't you worry, dear. We won't let them get away with this."

How could we possibly stop an anonymous attack like this, I wondered?

I had never felt more defeated than I did in that moment. Having lost the will to fight, I could only stand there and stare. Even though Nathanial had removed the signs, their words had been freshly seared into my mind.

"I'm more convinced that we are making the right decision by you coming to stay with us," Irene said. "What if you had been home when all this happened? Who knows what they might have done..."

"Everything seems fine out back," Nathanial said, reappearing around the corner of the cottage. "Nothing more than some unruly weeds in the flowerbed." He tried to smile at me, but I couldn't quite muster the same in reply.

"Come along, Nathanial," Irene said. "Let's get Helen back to the house so she can rest."

Not much was said on the way back to their home. Nathanial and Irene discussed plans for dinner, on which I felt like I was imposing, but I hardly heard anything they were saying to one another.

Everything seemed to be moving in a blur around me.

All I could think about were those signs fixed to my door, and in the yard...

"Helen, dear, why don't you go ahead and take a nice, long bath before dinner?" Irene asked me as we arrived back at their house. She helped me out of the cumbersome jacket I'd chosen to wear when I went to investigate Lucas Adams, setting it on the back of one of the chairs in the dining room. "Maybe it will help you relax a little."

"Perhaps I will," I said, smiling a tight smile at her. "If it's all right with you. I could very well help with dinner."

"You can help with dinner as soon as you are all refreshed," Irene said. "Now go, please. You've had a hard enough day as it is."

In truth, I found the exhaustion was beginning to catch up with me. As I sunk into the frothy, warm water, sleepiness made my eyelids droop, and I fought yawn after yawn as I massaged my weary muscles.

You've had a hard day as it is.

In my recent life, it seemed that I was having more hard days than easy ones. Admittedly, though, the days seemed to be getting harder and harder as time passed. In a way, I would have given almost anything to go back in time to when I was only looking through the clues that might point me in the direction of what had happened to my aunt. Somehow, things had seemed simpler back then.

Now people were leaving terrible messages on my front door, intended to frighten me and make me feel remorse for something I hadn't even done...for a murder I never committed.

My world felt as if it were becoming smaller now, and especially small was the list of those who I could definitely trust. Irene, Nathanial, and Sam Graves. Enough to count on one hand.

I sunk down beneath the water, blowing frustrated bubbles from my lips. Those were not great numbers, especially when anyone in this village could have been the one to kill Mr. James...

It made little sense, and if anything, made me feel as if everything in my life was coming to a head. *Things can't get any worse than they are now...right?* I thought.

My father once told me to never tempt fate. Never say never. He said that most of the time, the way we responded to events in our lives was more about perspective than the actual events themselves.

Maybe that was how I had to look at this whole thing. Perhaps if I could just change my response to it, become more proactive than reactive, then everything might turn out differently.

There was no way to be certain...except to try.

I pulled the plug at the bottom of the tub, watching as the water swirled around in a vortex, disappearing down the drain. The evening air brushed against my flushed, damp skin, chilling me, and waking me up.

I couldn't wallow in self-pity. That wasn't helpful to anyone, and I certainly was not going to get any further in my investigations by allowing myself to be troubled by what some angry people had to say.

It took more willpower than anger to force the images from my mind, but as I dressed in an outfit that Irene had found for me, I determined that I was not going to think about the signs any longer, and would focus instead on finding the murderer so I could go back to living my life.

Besides...if we find the real killer, than perhaps those people will apologize for ever saying such terrible things, I thought hopefully.

I wandered out into the kitchen, where the heady scent of garlic filled the air.

"Something smells wonderful," I said as I ran a brush through the ends of my hair, my towel draped over my shoulder to catch the falling droplets of bath water.

Irene, who stood at the stove, swiveled her head to smile at me. "I'd hoped so. Would you like to help me peel the carrots and potatoes?"

"I'd be happy to," I said, setting the brush and towel down into one of the kitchen chairs.

I stepped up to the counter, finding the station and ingredients all ready for me. I knew this was a simple task that Michael could have done had he been home, but I appreciated Irene's desire to give me something to do with my hands so that I didn't feel entirely helpless.

"How was the bath?" she asked.

"Just what I needed, really," I said. "I think it helped me to realize that I needed to not focus on the signs, and instead focus on the case itself."

"That's good," Irene said. "You know, it was probably the work of just one busybody who had far too much time on his or her hands."

"I understand, in a way..." I said. "Mr. James was not just some random citizen here in the village. He was a prominent figure, well loved by all, including me. It's devastating to think that something so horrific happened to him, which is why I want to help get to the bottom of it. Even though the people in the village want to think they know the truth, the reality is that they don't, and I just have to accept that." I picked up the thin knife Irene had set out for me, and began to peel the carrot nearest to me, which was rather fat around the stem. "My father told me all the time when I was young that, often times, our experiences are more about our responses, instead of the situations themselves. It's very easy to react to something going wrong, but what is more important is that we choose to react well. Does that make sense?"

"Very much so," Irene said. "What do you plan to do next, then? You have the Inspector following up about the mechanic, yes?"

"Yes," I said. "Though I'm not entirely confident in that. Part of me wonders if I was just so desperate to find the person who killed the vicar that I latched onto the first thing that even remotely looked like a lead."

"Are you rethinking your earlier assessment, then?" she asked.

I finished peeling that first carrot, and began to slice it into narrow discs. "I don't know," I said. "He was so unwilling to speak to me about anything, that I cannot be sure of what his intentions were at all, if he had any in the first place. You see, when I asked him about Mr. James, he immediately became cold and angry, and didn't want to talk about it any further."

"That's not a normal reaction," Irene said as she poured some turkey stock into a pot on the stove. "It is definitely suspicious."

"Maybe yes, maybe no," I said, upending the cutting board with the diced carrots into the bowl Irene had set aside for me before picking up another to peel. "If what you said earlier is true, though, and he'd had a romantic involvement with Mr. James' daughter but was then forbidden from seeing her again...that would certainly leave behind feelings of resentment, especially if the relationship had been serious in nature."

"That is true, I suppose," Irene said. "What exactly did he say to you?"

"Very little," I said. "He told me he had made his peace with what happened, and that his connection with the family had long since passed."

"But the boots – " Irene said.

"That was a bit of a stretch, even I'll admit," I said. "That sort of mud can be found down by the river, since there is so much clay along the banks and in the riverbed itself. It might just be a coincidence that it also happens to be the same sort of mud that is mixed in with the dirt up near the churchyard…"

Irene pursed her lips. "Why do you seem determined to throw away the first good lead you've had?"

"Because I'm not certain it really is a lead in the first place," I said. "I can't explain it, but it…I don't know. It doesn't quite sit right with me. In all honesty, it makes me wonder if I'm back at square one, and if I should just keep looking. The question would be…where? Who can I trust?"

Irene gave me a sidelong look out of the corner of her grey eyes.

"I know I can trust you," I said. "But we followed the lead that you suggested. For now, it has brought us to a dead end."

"For now," Irene said.

I dumped some more peeled carrots into the bowl, which Irene then picked up and overturned into the pot of now simmering broth.

"Perhaps your best option would be to call Sam Graves

once again," Irene said. "That way you can see if he found out anything about Lucas Adams today."

"I doubt he would have had time already," I said. "But I thought about calling him anyways, to see if someone could watch my house through all of this. Sam won't be very happy to hear that someone vandalized it like they did."

"That's probably a good idea," Irene said.

"The truth is, I don't think there is anyone in the village that I could ask for help if I wanted to," I said. "It's incredibly frustrating, but for now, everyone is going to see me as nothing more than a suspect."

Irene sighed, dipping her wooden spoon into the broth and giving it a gentle mix. "Indeed. I've heard far too many nasty rumors. I suppose I always do, but I never in all my life thought I would hear them about you."

I smiled at her. "That is kind of you to say," I said. "What I need to do now is to find someone who was embittered toward the church, but also toward Mr. James himself."

"Unfortunately, that could be a great many people," Irene said. "People find reasons to get angry at God all the time, and end up leaving the church for rather ridiculous reasons."

"I know," I said. "Which is going to make this task of finding the real killer that much more difficult."

9

Irene and I agreed that first thing in the morning, I was going to speak with Inspector Graves. All of the determination I had felt seemed strong enough. I had never second guessed myself before.

In the morning, though...I began to doubt whether or not it was the right time to speak with him yet.

"But you were so convinced he could help last night," Irene said as I helped her spread fresh tablecloths over the tables down in the tea room. "What changed your mind?"

"I think he would have tried to contact me if he learned anything about Lucas," I said. "And to be quite honest, I don't think I could bring myself to walk back into the police station. Not yet."

"You could always call him," Irene said.

"Yes, but I would have to speak with that wretched secretary first," I said. "The one who spread all those rumors about Sam and me being together?"

Irene sighed, shaking her head as she smoothed the wrinkles from the tablecloth she'd just laid down. "I understand your reluctance, but if this would help you to find the culprit sooner – ”

“I'm not convinced it would,” I said. “I just think it would be wasting his time.”

“What about the vandalism to your home?” she asked. “Wouldn't that be enough to get him to do something?”

“Perhaps,” I said. “But even still, I would feel as if I was imposing on him.”

“What do you plan to do, instead?” Irene asked.

“Something I probably should have done the morning after Mr. James was killed,” I said. “I think in my fear it completely slipped my mind. I need to go and examine the place where he was killed.”

Irene stopped, giving me a startled look. “Helen, you cannot be serious,” she said. “Won't the police be watching it?”

“Not anymore,” I said. “At least, probably not. If anything, it might be roped off.”

“Won't someone see you?” she asked.

“I have that disguise,” I said. “I'll wear it and say I was coming to pay my respects.”

Irene did not seem convinced that it was a wise idea, but I'd set my heart on it. “Besides, if I find some more clues, then maybe I can bring a clearer story to Sam, making it even more unlikely that I was the killer in the first place. Maybe I'll find a footprint, or a scrap of fabric. Who knows?”

“Wouldn't the police have found that when they were doing their own investigations in the area?” she asked.

“Perhaps,” I said. “But they may have been more concerned about the body at that point in time. It couldn't hurt. And it will keep me out of people's way. I promise I won't dawdle. When I get back, I'll help you in the kitchen again."

"That's not why I was worried about you going..." Irene said.

I got ready after that in the same disguise as the one I'd worn when I went to see Lucas Adams. I tied my hair back, draped the same silk scarf around my neck. The sunglasses came in handy, as well, since the sun was so bright that Saturday morning.

As I made my way to the stairs, I pulled the hat over my face, keeping the brim low so as to hide my features. It had worked fairly well the last time I'd worn it. Irene simply knew me too well to be fooled.

"Be careful," she urged me as she laid out the teapots beside the stove in the kitchen downstairs, the shop ten minutes from opening.

"I will," I said, and slipped out into the morning.

At once, I regretted the jacket. The air was humid, and the thick, puffy clouds overhead indicated that rain was imminent that afternoon. I would have been much happier in a light dress with capped sleeves and a thin sweater.

Too bad all those clothes were back at my house. I made a mental note to ask Nathanial to go with Irene to fetch a few new outfits for me. I was growing tired of wearing the same thing day in and day out.

I walked down High Street, which was bustling as usual on Saturday. School was going to be back in session soon enough, and the children seemed to be doing all they could to make the most of the few days of freedom they had left, choosing to spend their time outdoors from the time the sun came up until it went back down again.

A man in a suit wandered past, his hand clutching a

briefcase with worn corners and a long scratch across the front. He tipped his hat at me as he passed, not slowing his quick gait.

I continued down the street, acting as if I, too, had somewhere important to be.

The cemetery came into view a short time later, the wrought iron fence lining the side of the street, the lonely headstones dotting the landscape beyond.

My stomach twisted into knots as memories of the night I'd found Mr. James in there came rushing back, as clear as if they had just happened.

I hovered near the entrance, staring up the dirt path leading further inside.

I took a deep breath, my heart beating uncomfortably in my chest, and stepped through.

I could have made my way to the place where Mr. James had died with my eyes closed. In my dreams, I'd run through the graves every night since it happened. I felt myself almost drawn toward the spot, as if the tree where I'd found him was a magnet, lulling me in its direction against my will.

When I reached the ancient tree, I let out a breath I hadn't realized I'd been holding.

He isn't there, I told myself. *His body won't be there.*

No, it wouldn't be. I knew that. But in my mind...that was a different story.

I stepped around the tree, and was faintly surprised at how ordinary the area looked.

I wasn't sure if I had expected blood, or a weapon lying there on the ground, or Mr. James' glasses, cast off in the struggle for his life. None of those things were there.

The dirt around the base of the tree seemed to be

disturbed, but no more than the paths nearby, or any different than any of the other trees I'd passed. The grass had already started to grow once again in the area, and there wasn't anything like a gash in the tree, or a stain in the bark.

Nothing could be seen that indicated it was the place where Mr. James had met his end...and returned home to be with the Lord.

I laid my hand against the tree, my knees suddenly weak. I could still smell the tang of his blood, feel the fear in his eyes as he stared up at me, unfocused.

I clutched at my heart which felt like it might beat right out of my chest.

I turned away, holding the tree for support, taking great gulps of air, trying to stop the shaking in my hands and legs.

It took me a few moments to gather myself, but there was nothing there to see. There wasn't even any police tape, which I had fully expected to see. Nothing to indicate that a man had died here.

I wasn't sure if I should be relieved or saddened because of that.

I started toward the main entrance near the front of the church, not wanting to go back through the same side gate that I'd entered through before, in case anyone had been watching. I hoped that people would have thought nothing of me, lingering near the churchyard, debating about going within.

My strength returned with every step I took away from the tree. It had been harder than I expected, going to visit that spot. In all the murders I'd experienced since arriving in Brookminster, I had never felt so distraught by a death. The beggar had saddened me, certainly, as had the widow who had reminded me of myself. But the vicar had died in front of me. I had to experience the death with him, be the last to see him alive. That was a privilege that not even his family had...and I carried it around like a stone in the pit of my stomach.

I checked to make sure the scarf and hat I wore were properly covering my face before I stepped out into the street once again, much nearer to the church than before.

It would be easy enough to head back to the teahouse without being seen. I imagined that most people would have moved on with their days, not worrying much about a woman who was wandering about.

At least...that was what I hoped for.

Feeling discouraged, I turned to head back to Irene, to tell her what little information I'd found, when a voice across the street caught my attention.

"You're not the first one curious about his death..."

I stopped in my tracks, wondering for a moment if I'd heard correctly or not.

I shifted my gaze across the street to a little rundown cottage at the end of the street, dwarfed in size by well-maintained homes on either side.

The man who had spoken stood in his front garden, clutching a cane that seemed to wobble as he leaned upon it. He'd just risen from a rickety, wooden chair that looked as if it might fall apart at any moment. He was scrawny in the arms and legs, but a round belly protruded from his middle, the buttons bulging somewhat.

"Been about a dozen folk streaming in and out of there, pretending to go visit the graves of loved ones, or taking a shortcut. Bah..." he said in a raspy, tired voice. "We all know they just wanted to see the exact place where he died."

I blinked a few times, wondering again if I'd heard him correctly.

"I'm sorry, are you speaking to me?" I asked.

"Who else would I be talking to?" he asked, his bushy, grey eyebrows coming together in a wrinkled line across his forehead. "The sky? The trees? They're not very good company."

Oh goodness, I thought. *This man may very well not have all of his marbles.*

"I was right, though, wasn't I?" the man asked. "You're not the first one. There have been a lot of people wandering around here lately, same as you, checking over their shoulder to make sure they haven't been followed. I've seen those guilty looks."

For a moment, I considered denying what it was I'd been doing in there. It surprised me just how accurate the man was, how easily he had seen through me.

He's seen others wandering around through here...I wonder if he saw the killer?

I glanced up and down the street, checking to make sure there were no cars or bicycles coming, and hurried over to the old man's gate into his front garden.

From this close, I realized that it must have been some time since the man had taken care of his belongings. Every corner of the yard was cluttered with some mess; old terracotta potters, an old push mower, a rusted trio of buckets...

The lawn itself was ratty as well, overgrown along the outside of the house, and along the base of the wild looking elm tree growing in the side yard. A wheelbarrow stood off to the side, laden with dirt and weeds, a pair of rubber gloves draped over the handlebars.

"A lot of people have been going to pay their respects, then?" I asked the man.

The man grunted in reply. "Pay their respects? Weren't you listening to a word I said? They were coming to see where he died. Wanted to see if they could spook themselves by seeing his ghost or some such nonsense."

"What sort of people?" I asked.

The man shifted his weight, his cane wobbling again. "Who might be asking? You aren't with the police, are you?"

"No," I said. "My name is Penelope Driscoll. I'm Nathanial's cousin."

"I see," the man said. "Thought you might be working for Inspector Graves, with that get up you have on." The stiffness of his stance seemed to lessen. "Name's Barty Grey."

I self-consciously touched the scarf wrapped around my neck. *Doesn't like the idea of the police snooping around, hmm?* "Have they been coming around often? The police, I mean," I asked.

"Every day, it seems," he said. "Not surprising, though. I imagine they want to find whoever it is that killed Mr. James."

My heart skipped as I glanced over my shoulder up at the church. It seemed so pretty, so cheerful even, bathed in the warm sunlight. I said, "I heard it was that Helen woman, the one who used to spend so much time with that murderer Sidney Mason." Stoking the flames of the fire may prove fruitless, but it was clear he didn't recognize me in this disguise. I wondered if he would have recognized me, anyway.

The man shook his head. "I've heard the same thing, but wasn't she the one who cleared her aunt's name as well? Found out that Mrs. Martin had been bribing and blackmailing customers? She doesn't strike me as the type to do that, not with that sort of self-righteous behavior."

I opened my mouth to agree with his generosity, but as his last comment sunk in, a defense rose to my lips, and I just barely managed to swallow it before outright challenging him.

Self-righteous? Me? If only he knew what I had to go through in order to get the information I was looking for...

"So who do you think did it, then?" I asked, as casually as I could with flushed cheeks. "Has anyone walking around the churchyard seemed suspicious lately?"

Barty's gaze shifted over my shoulder, peering into the front garden of the church. "Well, unfortunately, that could have been anyone, really. As I said, there have been many who have done exactly what you did. Though I'm not certain that a killer would have returned to that spot, even if they were curious about what happened to the body. Too risky."

"Risky, indeed," I said, folding my arms. "It's all so very strange, though, isn't it? The poor man, killed in broad daylight, and no one can seem to find out who did it. It's all anyone in the village can speak of." That was the truth, of course. Irene had told me that she heard it mentioned at nearly every table in the teahouse at least once during the last few days.

"That's what I've heard..." Barty said, shaking his head. "I'll be happy when it's all put to bed, I tell you. All this commotion is not good for my heart."

"Yes, I can see how it might be disturbing," I said.

I wanted to continue to ask questions of this man, but was not certain as to whether it would produce any sound clues.

"Have you seen anyone come around here more than once?" I asked.

"You seem awfully interested for someone who isn't helping the police," Barty said with a slight edge to his words.

"I'm simply curious," I said. "I certainly did not mean to offend."

"You haven't," Barty said heavily. "I'm just tired of answering these questions, is all."

"You're simply the first person I've met who seems to know more than anyone else."

"I don't know anything more than anyone," he said, somewhat hotly. "How could I? All I've seen is people coming in and out of there. No one's talked to me, not really. Not except the police, asking if I saw anything the day Mr. James was killed…"

My eyes widened. "Did you?"

"No," Barty said heavily, with apparent disappointment. "No, I didn't. But I wish I had."

Silence fell between us, making me look back at the church and the cemetery beyond, wondering what secrets it held that I just couldn't quite figure out.

"It is a pity, really…" I said. "Mr. James was such a nice fellow."

The man grunted. "Everybody has a past, though. I know it makes me unpopular, but I always thought something was strange about him. I never could trust him, myself."

I stared at the man, finding myself surprised. He was certainly right; that would be seen as an unpopular opinion among the townsfolk. "But he was so kind," I said. "So generous with his time and energy."

Barty slowly lowered himself back down into his chair, his knuckles nearly white from gripping his cane for support. "Perhaps," he said. "But people like him always struck me as fake. No one could be like that all the time. Not even a man of God."

I frowned. "That's a rather cynical view of the world. You remind me of someone I know who would likely agree with you."

The man's face split into a reluctant smirk. "I'm not proud of my cynicism, Miss. But years of people breaking their promises and turning on each other tends to make you think less of those around you."

I could understand what he meant, which surprised me. "I...think I know what you mean," I said.

The man let out a hollow laugh. "You're too young to know what I mean."

The church bells began to chime, then, signaling the noon hour.

"My apologies, Miss Driscoll, but these old bones require more rest than they used to," Barty said, struggling to his feet. "If you'll excuse me, I think I'll go have some tea."

"Oh, certainly," I said. "Thank you for answering a young lady's curious inquiries, Mr. Grey."

He dipped his head. "I'd say it was my pleasure, but murder is unsavory business, isn't it?"

"Indeed it is," I said, watching him as he wandered back to his front door. "Indeed it is."

10

I tried not to run all the way back to the teahouse. Very nearly dancing with my nerves all in a bundle, it became difficult for me to remain calm as I chewed on the events that had just transpired.

While there had been no obvious evidence at the scene of the crime, there had been one rather crotchety old man who seemed to have a great dislike for Mr. James. Of course, his dislike seemed to make some semblance of sense, given he had provided a reason, though somewhat vague, for not trusting the vicar.

Regardless, I now felt that I had grounds to speak with Sam Graves. Between the old man, the lack of evidence at the site of the death, the vandalism of my home, and curiosity about what Sam had found, if anything, about Lucas Adams, it was time to give him another call.

"Go on ahead and use the phone," Irene said when I pulled her aside upon arriving back at the teahouse. "Do you plan to go down to the station?"

"No," I said. "I'm going to use another false name when I

call so I don't run into any trouble with the receptionist like I did before."

"Fair enough," Irene said. "If Inspector Graves wishes to discuss these matters in person, why don't you see if he wants to come for dinner tonight? That would provide a place to speak without any unwanted ears listening in."

Thinking her idea was a good one, I made my way upstairs, sat myself down beside the telephone, and dialed the number for the police station.

Heart beating rapidly, I waited for someone to answer the other line.

"Brookminster Law Enforcement office," said the nasally voice of the receptionist, Rachel, on the other end.

Goosebumps appeared on my skin in a wave, making my head spin. I cleared my throat, and putting on the best accent I could, picked up the persona I'd used when speaking to Mrs. Georgianna, mimicking Sidney's Scottish accent. "Yes, hello, might I speak to Inspector Graves, please?"

"I'm sorry, but Inspector Graves is very busy, and has asked to not be disturbed," Rachel said in a flat, uninterested tone, though lacking the hostility that she seemed to save exclusively for me. It seemed my guise was working.

"I imagine he is quite busy," I said. "But this matter is very important, and of a sensitive nature. I am out of town, otherwise I would come down to speak with him at once."

An exasperated sigh made my blood start to boil. Was she truly that put out by my request? "I'll see what I can do, but I cannot make any promises. One moment, please."

I bit down on the end of my thumbnail as I waited. That woman was utterly infuriating sometimes. What was she doing that was so much more important than her job?

Painting her nails? Smoking yet another cigarette? Gossiping with Paige?

I certainly wouldn't put it past her.

Nearly five minutes went by before I heard the rustling of the receiver, and she spoke again. "Inspector Graves would like to know who it is that is disturbing him when he so clearly asked not to be," Rachel said. "His words exactly, I'm afraid."

I bit my tongue so hard the metallic tang of blood coated my mouth. "Tell him I'm his old friend from that case about the German spy a while back...the one involving a decorated war hero's wife?"

"No name, Miss?" Rachel asked in a scathing tone.

"Yes, you can give him my name," I said. "Miss Klein. Daughter of General Klein."

"O – oh, my apologies," Rachel said, all disdain fleeing from her tone. She may not have known the name but she was obviously impressed by the rank. "I am terribly sorry for my behavior. Let me go get the Inspector at once."

A distinct *click* followed her words, and I was left sitting in silence for a few moments.

"A bit risky, isn't it? Calling down here under a false name like that," Sam said when he picked up the other end of the line.

"How did you know it was me?" I asked.

"Need I remind you what my profession is?" Sam asked with a low chuckle. "Though Rachel certainly had no idea it was you, so I suppose your undercover skills are improving."

"I've had a great deal of practice as of late..." I said, somewhat bitterly.

"What happened now?" Sam asked.

"Too much to explain over the telephone," I said. "I was

wondering if we could possibly meet so we could discuss these things I've found out without being overheard?"

"Let me take a look at my schedule," he said, and I heard rustling papers on the other end. "I have a meeting at half past three, but should be done before five. Where would you like to meet?"

"Irene told me to invite you over to their house for dinner this evening," I said.

"Are you staying with them?" Sam asked.

"For the time being," I said. "Irene is worried that I am not safe alone in my home...and to be honest, I'm starting to believe her."

"Why do you say that?" he asked.

"I'll let you know when you get here," I said, not wanting someone to overhear his end of the conversation.

"Very well," Sam said with a heavy sigh. "I will come by for dinner. What time should I arrive? Six? Seven?"

"Six should be fine," I said. "That will give us a chance to speak before we eat."

"I'll bring something for dessert," he said. "Stop by the bakery on my way over and find something."

I spent the rest of the afternoon in the kitchen of the teahouse, anxiously waiting for the evening to come. I dutifully cleaned all of the cups that came back in, prepared the tea, and arranged the tea cakes on their floral china plates just so, adding some doilies that Irene had knit to the trays before sending them on their way with Nathanial.

When we closed the tea shop, Irene and Nathanial were exhausted, so I offered to make dinner.

"You don't have to do that," Irene said. "You worked all day, too."

"Please, it's all right," I said. "Besides, I'm the reason we are having company for dinner in the first place."

"We're having company?" Nathanial asked, wiping his forehead with a handkerchief as we made our way up the stairs to their flat.

"Oh, honey, I'm sorry," Irene said. "Inspector Graves will be joining us for dinner."

"Oh, the inspector..." Nathanial said. "How wonderful."

"I'm sorry..." I said. "I promise, we will keep our conversation brief."

"No, no, it's all right," Nathanial said, rubbing the back of his neck. "I'm certain that we will have plenty of times in the future where our dining table isn't filled with conversations about murder and death..."

Guilt began to well up within me until Nathanial laid a hand on my shoulder.

"I'm joking," he said, with a warm smile. "It's all right. If it's what is needed to clear your name, then it's no trouble."

Feeling better overall, I got to work making dinner. I chose something simple, a shepherd's pie.

"I thought the men might appreciate a filling meal," I told Irene as I hefted the cast iron into the oven to keep warm and brown the potatoes. "Especially if we are going to be talking about Mr. James."

Irene nodded. "It smells delicious. I'm sure they'll be pleased."

A tiny face appeared around the corner of the hallway, sniffing the air eagerly. "Mum? When's dinner?" Michael asked, his grey eyes wide with anticipation.

"Very soon, honey," Irene said. "I think we might feed you first so you can get outside and play before the sun goes down."

Michael's face brightened. "Can I go play with Samuel if he's outside?"

Irene's lips pursed, and I watched as she half rolled her eyes. "Couldn't Samuel come and play with you tonight, instead?"

"But Mum, he has that new slide," Michael said. "And who knows how much longer we have to play in his pond before school starts again."

"Oh, that blasted pond..." Irene said, planting her hands on her hips. "No, no pond tonight. I don't want you coming home soaking wet."

"But Mum!" Michael whined.

"No," Irene said, walking across to him and steering him back down the hall. "Either he comes here and you play marbles or jacks, or you don't get to go out and play at all."

I smiled as I heard his indecipherable complaining disappearing as they went into his room.

I heard voices coming from up the stairs, and soon recognized them as Inspector Graves and Nathanial. They were talking about business around the village in a very polite, formal manner.

"Oh, something smells good," Inspector Graves said as he stepped up into the kitchen, looking around as eagerly as Michael had.

He spotted me near the stove, and a smile crossed over his face.

"Dinner is very nearly ready," I said, pulling open the oven and peering inside. The heat brushed against my face as I inspected the top of the potatoes. "Perhaps another five or so minutes."

We all sat down at the table together. Nathanial kindly hefted the large shepherd's pie I'd made and set it down in the middle of the table. Irene served Michael first, who didn't even seem to mind that it was steaming hot. We said grace, and everyone eagerly dove into their meal.

"This is delicious," Irene said, giving me an appreciative grin. "How did you get the meat to be so flavorful?"

"I don't know," I said. "I just did it the way that my grandmother taught me when I was a little girl."

"What sort of spices did you add?" Irene asked.

"Only what you have here," I said. "Salt, ground peppercorn, some parsley, and some paprika – "

"That must be it," Irene said, smiling at her husband. "Paprika. What a wonderful idea. It just makes it so much more flavorful."

"I'm done," Michael said, a smear of mashed potatoes streaked across his cheekbone. He slid down from his chair. "Can I go play outside now?"

Irene reached out and took his chin in one hand, and wiped her napkin across his cheek with the other. Then she kissed his forehead. "Very well," she said. "Make sure you are inside by half past eight."

"I will be!" Michael said, and he took off down the stairs.

Irene moved to clean her son's plate up as Nathanial glanced over his shoulder at the sound of Michael excitedly making a dash for the outside.

"Well, now that the young ears are absent," Irene said, glancing back and forth between Sam and I. "Feel free to move into the sitting room. I'll get some tea ready. And this delicious pie that the inspector brought."

We went into the next room, settling into our respective seats. Nathanial took his armchair beside the fire, and I took the padded bench beneath the window. Inspector Graves sat down on the far side of the sofa, his back rigid.

"Inspector, you are welcome to feel at home here," Irene said, bringing some glasses of cold water to the coffee table. "I promise you don't have to feel as if you are working."

"Thank you, Mrs. Driscoll," Sam said, but he didn't change his posture. "Thank you once again for having me over for a meal. It's been some time since I have eaten in a family setting."

"That's terrible," Irene said from the kitchen. "No one should have to eat alone."

"It's not out of choice, at least not usually," Sam said. "I'm often at the station well into the evening, filing paperwork or making phone calls."

"They work you too hard," Nathanial said, shaking his head. "Surely there are others who could take your shift some nights?"

"I certainly wish," Sam said. "It's the price I pay for the job I've chosen."

"I imagine this latest case has kept you busy," I said, giving him a concerned look.

He met my gaze, his eyes, piercing blue, reflecting the same concern. "Yes..." he said heavily. "Perhaps too busy. I haven't had much of a chance to breathe lately, much less get to follow up on the leads that I've wanted to."

"You haven't?" I asked.

He shook his head. "I'm sorry, Helen. I know you wanted me to speak with that mechanic, but the chief has had me working day and night on a different case all together."

"What?" I asked. "What sort of case?"

"Can't share that," Sam said, looking down at his hands knotted in his lap. "I'm sorry, but it's nothing all that serious, and it doesn't involve you at all. It's ridiculous, if you ask me, entirely a waste of my time, especially when a murderer is still out there on the loose."

I realized he wasn't looking at me when he said that. I said, "All of the police think I did it, don't they? All of them but you?"

Sam's brief glance up at me said everything for him.

I sighed with exasperation. "Well, they will certainly be surprised when they find out that they, like everyone else, are wrong."

"Yes, they will be," Sam said. "So why don't you tell me exactly what you've learned about this case so that we can move forward?"

I shifted on the bench I sat on, my nerves twinging. "Well...I'd hoped you had a chance to go and check out Lucas Adams," I said. "Though I'm not entirely certain he's our killer. Too many coincidences. However, when I went to the cemetery to search the area where Mr. James' body had been, I ran into an elderly gentleman who lives across from the church. His name was Barty Grey."

"Barty Grey," Nathanial said. "I know him. He's quite an ornery man, isn't he?"

"Yes," I said. "And he seems to have disliked Mr. James."

Sam folded his arms, his thick, dark brow furrowing. "Did he?" he asked. "All right, tell me what you learned."

"He told me that he had seen quite a few people wandering around the cemetery," I said. "That's how he noticed me. Called out to me, telling me I wasn't the first one curious about the vicar's death."

"He said that?" Irene asked. "What gall."

"That's what I thought," I said. "But he was completely right. That was precisely what I was doing over there. It seems that there have been many others, pretending to visit the graves of loved ones or simply taking a stroll...he said he wasn't fooled, though, knowing they were going to see where the body had been."

"That's quite morose," Nathanial said.

"Did he mention names?" Sam asked.

I shook my head. "No," I said. "I even asked if he'd noticed certain people showing up more than once. He insisted that if someone had killed Mr. James, they likely wouldn't return to the place where he'd been killed, out of fear of being caught."

"I'm not sure I entirely agree," Sam said. "Some people are so driven by guilt that they can't help but go back and make sure their tracks have been covered, sometimes literally."

"That's what I would have thought," Nathanial said. "Interesting that he didn't name any names, though."

"He said that he didn't think I did it," I said.

"That could have been flattery," Sam said.

"No," I said. "I was disguised, and claimed to be Penelope Driscoll, Nathanial's cousin."

Nathanial straightened. "I didn't realize I had a cousin Penelope."

"Well, now you do," I said. "In case someone asks after her."

Nathanial nodded, worry creasing his brow.

"You weren't lying when you said you've had your fair share of practice lately," Sam said.

"Precisely," I said.

"And you said that he didn't like Mr. James?" Irene asked, reappearing with a tray of steaming teacups, setting it down beside the water that none of us had touched yet.

"That's rather odd, isn't it? How could someone not like that wonderful man?"

"He didn't seem to despise him," I said. "He just seemed to think that he was simply pretending. He said that no one can be that kind and compassionate. He said that everyone has a past, and that he wasn't sure he could trust someone who seemed as fake as Mr. James."

"That's a matter of opinion," Nathanial said. "Did he even know him?"

I shrugged. "I have no idea." I looked over at Sam. "He did say that years of watching people break their promises and turn their backs on one another led him to a rather cynical view of the world, and may have contributed to his rather troubling view."

Sam sighed, looking down. "Unfortunately, I can understand that mentality. I wonder if he ever worked in police or government in some capacity."

"I don't know…" I said. "I should have asked."

"So is this man a suspect, then?" Irene asked, wiping her hands on the apron that she'd put on. "Or just a source of information?"

"I suppose anyone with any form of motive should be considered as a suspect," Sam said, pinching the bridge of his nose. "Though to be honest, none of the suspects we've unearthed yet seem to meet the criteria for murder. Simple dislike or coincidences are weak, at best. What we need is someone with real motive, or even a real connection to Mr. James…"

He glanced over at me.

"Which is why I was wondering if you'd gone to speak with the family yet."

I blinked at him. "Me? Why?"

"Because that is what you do, isn't it?" he asked. "You seek out the ties to the victims and find a way to talk with them. This time, though, you haven't gone to see the family. Why?"

"Well, for one, I thought you already have?" I asked.

"I did," he said. "But even still, I'm curious as to why you didn't."

"I haven't been able to leave the house, much less speak with anyone with the scarlet letter painted across my chest," I said. "And I am quite certain that his family would absolutely despise the sight of me, especially given the fact that I am the primary suspect for Mr. James' murder as of now."

Sam nodded. "Well, I suppose that does make sense. Yet you went and talked to the mechanic who had been seeing his daughter at one point in time?"

"Yes," I said. "But as I said, I'm not entirely sure that was a fruitful errand. You see, I think he might be innocent."

"But you don't know that for sure," Irene said. "Those boots – "

"What boots?" Sam asked.

"I didn't tell you when we spoke?" I asked. "I found a pair of boots covered in the same type of mud that makes up the ground of the cemetery when I went snooping around the mechanic's place."

"That's good evidence, isn't it?" Irene asked.

"It would be, if the same sort of clay wasn't also in the riverbeds all along the outskirts of the city," I said.

"She's right," Sam said. "It could point right to him as the killer, or it could mean nothing at all. I hadn't realized you had found something like that. However...I still am rather suspicious about Mr. James' daughter. Especially after how she evaded me when I went to see her and the rest of the family."

"She evaded you?" I asked. "Why? Wouldn't she realize that would make her more suspicious?"

"Perhaps not," he said. "I didn't think much of it at the time, given the fact that everyone was grieving, and I felt as if I was intruding while they were preparing for a funeral they never saw coming."

"I wonder if we were to speak to her about Lucas Adams, maybe she would be able to give us more information than what he gave me?" I asked.

"It's not a bad assumption," Sam said. "My plan was to go and follow-up with the family sometime in the next few days, especially when the funeral is upon us."

"They finally set a date?" I asked.

"Seems so," Sam said. "Would you be interested in going with me? Perhaps underneath one of your disguises?"

I brightened. "You'd be all right with that?" I asked.

"I wouldn't have suggested it otherwise," he said. "I realize that you want to get your name cleared, and that's what I want, too. I...saw what happened to your home. The names, the writing on the signs...those sorts of terrible things. The sooner we can figure this whole mess out, the better for everyone."

I set my jaw, my eyes narrowing. "When do we meet with the family?"

"Tomorrow at ten," Sam said. "And make sure you dress for a funeral."

11

I f anyone had told me a year ago that I'd be working alongside the police inspector of a small village to help solve a murder, I would have thought they were positively mad. Why in the world would someone like me ever get involved with something as atrocious as murder?

I also never would have thought I could end up as a suspect in a murder investigation, either...but I had been caught trying to help the victim, his blood all over my hands...

I checked my outfit in the mirror one last time, hoping that I did not look at all like myself.

Irene had given me a bottle of food coloring she would often use for decorating cakes and cookies, a vibrant red that reminded me far too much of fresh blood.

"If you wash some of this through your hair, it could give you a temporary dye for the investigation," she said. "It certainly wouldn't last very long, but it could be enough to keep them from recognizing you easily."

I'd stood in the shower for nearly an hour, deftly trying

to rub some of the food coloring through my chestnut hair, watching with mingled horror and fascination as the color ran through my fingers, and down the length of the tub to the drain. It stained the ends of my fingertips pink, leading me to decide to wear a pair of delicate black silk gloves.

After drying and styling my hair, I realized that it was considerably redder than it had been before. With a few swipes of my scissors as well, I trimmed my hair to my shoulders, curling the ends with some rollers, which was something I would not typically do for everyday wear.

I chose a darker red lipstick, and caked on the blush and eyeshadow, making sure to highlight my cheekbones. I painted dark, heavy lines around my eyes, and brushed on so much mascara that I thought my eyelashes must sound like the legs of a scurrying beetle whenever I blinked.

By the time I'd dressed in the same dress I'd worn for Roger's funeral, I was certain I would be unable to recognize myself.

How right I was.

Inspector Graves called me that morning, saying he would stop by the Driscoll's house to pick me up on our way down to the James' home.

"I'll be here," I told him, hearing footsteps behind me in the kitchen. "See you soon."

When I hung up and turned around, I found Irene standing there, gaping at me, her jaw nearly touching the floor.

"Helen..." she said, rather breathlessly. "You...you look so different."

Self-consciously, I reached up and touched the ends of my hair. It was quite a bit shorter than it had been the night before. I smiled sheepishly at her. "Do I look just terrible?"

"No, not at all," Irene said. "If I didn't know it was you staying here, I would have assumed one of our teahouse guests had wandered up here by mistake."

She walked over to me, staring at my hair.

"The dye seems to have done the trick," she said. "Though I'm certain it will wash out the next time you take a shower."

"Good," I said. "I feel as if I look too much like my sister now. Her hair is quite red, you know. I could likely pass as her twin."

"Well, I think you will be able to investigate this case without anyone recognizing you," Irene said. "Who did you say you were going to be portraying today?"

"I haven't made up my mind, yet..." I said. "Who could be believable enough that the James' would allow me entrance to their home alongside the inspector?"

"I imagine they won't question his decision," Irene said. "He is the police, after all."

Nathanial's voice called up the stairs a short time later. "The inspector just pulled up outside."

I glanced at Irene, who nodded at me. "You'll do just fine," she said, smiling in a reassuring way.

I hugged her before I started downstairs, keeping my hat pulled low over my face in case any of the patrons at the teahouse saw me.

I slipped into the passenger seat of the police car, pulling the door shut behind me.

When I looked over at Sam, whose eyes were as large as teacups, I blushed. "What's the matter?" I asked.

"Oh, it's you," he said, blinking at me. "For a moment, I was wondering if I should ask a young woman such as yourself why she felt the need to get into a police car."

"Irene was also surprised," I said, somewhat annoyed. "This disguise cannot be *that* good. I don't see why you both are lying to me like you are."

"Oh, on the contrary," he said, shifting the car into drive. "You look like a different woman all together."

"I'm uncertain as to whether or not I should take that as a compliment," I said, giving him a wry sidelong smile.

He returned it just as easily before we headed off through the village.

I was none too surprised when we pulled up outside a home that was right beside the church. A vicarage, no doubt, giving Mr. James direct access to the building whenever he needed it.

"It must be torture for his family to be living here right now..." I said as we got out of the car, staring up at the lovely, quiet home. "Knowing that he died so close by, and no one was around to help him..."

"Apart from you, that is," Sam said.

"Yes, and look how much good I did," I said.

"You did what you could," Sam said.

We walked up to the door, where Sam knocked on the polished, brass knocker that was in the shape of a wren.

A commotion was heard inside, followed by a woman's scolding voice. "Get down – no, I said get down, Lila. Please."

The *click* of the lock was soon followed by the door swinging inward, revealing a pretty middle-aged woman with dark hair cut around her ears. "Oh, Inspector Graves," she said, her leg pushing against something out of sight. "I didn't expect to see you so soon today."

"My apologies, Mrs. James," he said. "Are we too early?"

"No, it's all right," she said, ducking behind the door.

"Lila, *please*. I'm sorry, our dog has been a mess since Walter died...she thinks everyone coming to the door is him finally coming home."

My heart ached as a blonde Labrador poked her nose between Mrs. James' leg and the door, sniffing eagerly at the air. She couldn't possibly understand what was happening...

"I'm afraid I haven't met your associate," Mrs. James said, grabbing onto Lila's collar, holding her back from Sam and I.

"This is Penelope Driscoll," Sam said. "She is a cousin to Nathanial Driscoll. Lives in London, and works for the police department there. She is considering transferring here to our station, and I thought her expertise might prove useful in this case."

She gave me a rather peculiar look. "Oh, of course," she said, smiling politely up at me, though I noticed how it didn't quite reach her eyes. "Well, won't you come in?"

She moved aside to allow us through, and released Lila as soon as the door was shut behind her.

"I apologize for the mess," she said, grabbing a vase of flowers, one of several that sat on tables and chairs in the entryway. "Things have been a bit hectic around here."

"Never you worry, Mrs. James," Sam said. "I promised you we would get this case solved, and I never break my promises."

"That's a relief to hear, Inspector," she said. "Please, won't you come in here?"

She gestured for us to follow her into a sitting room, which was just as messy as the rest of the house. Clothing had been draped over the back of a handsome maroon wingback chair, and a desk in the corner was piled high with papers and books. The coffee table, cluttered with teacups and small plates and napkins, looked as if it was nothing more than a secondary place for kitchen dishes.

Mrs. James picked up a pair of dress shoes – men's shoes – from the sofa, brushed it off with the back of her hand, and patted the cushion. "Here you are, Inspector, Miss Driscoll."

Sam and I politely took the seat on the couch.

Mrs. James hurried to another chair opposite us, perching awkwardly on the edge of the cushion as if she might need to flee at any moment, her hands knotted tightly in her lap. "What can I do for you, Inspector? What have you found out about my husband's case?"

"Your husband was an influential man in town," Sam said. "With that sort of position, there are many connections to investigate."

"Are you saying you have found more possible suspects?" she asked, her pencil-thin eyebrows knitting as tightly together as her fingers. "But I thought there was only the one, that woman who just moved here some months ago – "

Sam shook his head, leaning forward. "I'm sorry, Mrs. James, but finding the killer won't be as easy as that. Mrs. Lightholder, while still remaining in town, is at the bottom of our suspect list."

"But they found her, over my husband's dead body, with his blood all over her hands – " Mrs. James said, her eyes beginning to bulge. She recovered quickly, though, taking in a deep breath through her nose, closing her eyes. "And you're telling me she isn't the one?"

"No," Sam said. "We...have some other leads we would like to investigate, but we needed some more information first."

"What sort of information?" Mrs. James asked.

"Is Rachel home?" Sam asked. "She was the one I didn't get to speak with very much when I was here last."

Mrs. James' brow furrowed further. "I don't see why you would need to speak to my children," she said. "Haven't they been through enough?"

"I realize they have suffered a great deal," Sam said. "But there may be information only they can help me with."

Mrs. James's piercing gaze fixed itself on Sam for a few moments, her hands wringing in her lap. "Rachel is home, yes," she said after a few heartbeats. "Shall I go retrieve her?"

"That would be good, yes," Sam said.

She rose from her seat and excused herself from the room.

Sam glanced over at me.

"She's hurting, clearly," I said.

"Yes, and she doesn't trust me, either," Sam said. "I don't blame her, though. She wants me to find answers, and the only thing I come back to her with is more questions."

"I can see how that would be infuriating..." I said.

"Indeed," Sam agreed.

A few minutes later, raised voices floated down from the floor above us.

Sam and I exchanged a concerned look.

It wasn't long before we heard stomping down the stairs, and a young woman appeared in the doorway, dressed entirely in black, attempting to wrangle a hooped earring through her left earlobe.

Sam rose to his feet. "Ah, Miss Rachel. Please, won't you join us – "

"I don't have anything to say to you," she snapped, glaring at him.

I noticed a redness in her eyes, and a puffiness around her face. She'd been crying, and recently.

"Rachel, sweetheart..." her mother said, appearing behind her, a stern frown etched onto her pretty face. "Remember, he's with the police."

Rachel reminded me a great deal of her father. She had the same lean frame as he did, but while she had the same eyes and the same nose, she lacked the general warmth that I always felt from Mr. James.

She folded her arms, rolling her eyes, and took a reluctant step into the room. "Fine," she snapped. "What do you want?"

"We just want to talk," Sam said in as gentle of a voice as he could. The effect was lost, however, as he shifted his weight and folded his arms. "I know this has been a very difficult time for you, losing your father."

Rachel's nose wrinkled, and her chin pointed upward slightly.

"Why don't you come and sit down with us?" I asked, waving her into the room. "We promise all we want to do is talk, so we can help find your father's – "

"He's dead," she said sharply, glaring at me with flashing eyes. "Nothing you do will bring him back, not even finding who killed him."

"That's true," I said. "But we can certainly find justice for you and your – "

"Who is this?" Rachel asked, her hip cocked as she pointed at me. "I don't remember her being here last time."

"She's an associate of mine from London," Sam said as

easily as if it were true. "She's agreed to help us with this case."

Rachel opened her mouth to snap back with something else, but Mrs. James stepped in. "Honey, please just answer their questions so they can be on their way."

Her back was turned, but I could feel the heat from the look the woman gave her daughter even from where I sat.

Rachel sniffed, and then took the seat her mother had been sitting in.

Sam resumed his own spot on the sofa beside me, clearing his throat, though the room was not without its tension.

I pulled the small pad of paper he'd given me from the pocket of my jacket, and poised the pen over it, ready to write.

"Very good," Sam said. "Rachel, I didn't get a chance to ask you some of the questions I asked the rest of your siblings when I was here last week."

She shrugged, her arms folded tightly over her thin frame. Her eyes were fixed on the ceiling. "And?" she asked.

"Well, how can I be certain that you didn't see or notice anything they might not have?" Sam asked. "Your insight might be just what we need to solve this case."

She shifted, crossing one leg over the other, her bony knees wobbling as she bounced in her seat. "I have no idea about anything my father did," she said. "We hadn't spoken much the last few years. He never approved of the decisions I made in my life. Neither of my parents did."

I glanced over at Mrs. James, who was hovering just inside the sitting room doorway. She didn't seem surprised to hear her daughter say something so crass, yet she didn't seem unharmed by it, either.

"But you've been living here in Brookminster again for some time, haven't you?" Sam asked.

"Yes," Rachel said flatly. "Why is that important?"

"Was there anything strange going on the night that your father died?" he asked. "Perhaps you saw someone acting suspicious? Or perhaps you have heard something strange from someone since then?"

I could see he was fishing for information about the mechanic. I watched her face as well, looking for any hint of surprise, or reluctance to answer.

"Are you implying that I know people who would want to kill my father?" she asked.

"No," Sam said. "I asked your siblings these same questions. I'm sorry if they are bringing up unpleasant memories, but they could very well be important to our investigation."

She scoffed, rolling her eyes like a spoiled child. "No, I didn't see or hear anything suspicious," she said. "Can I leave now?"

It struck me how rude Rachel was being. I expected to see a grieving daughter, not some annoyed child who didn't seem at all interested in helping us find her father's killer.

"Not yet," Sam said. "Do you know of anyone who might have had an issue with your father?"

She snorted, which drew a nasty look from her mother. "There were plenty of people who didn't like my father," she said. "Oh, everyone in the village pretended to love him, but he was the one who told them from the pulpit every Sunday morning that they were supposed to live pure, good lives. Well, for some people, that sort of life is *boring*. And he always talked about how people are sinful, and you know what? Sometimes people just don't want to hear about that.

So, yes, there were people who didn't like him," she said. "Would you like a list? I'm certain we would be here all night."

"Rachel!" her mother snapped. "That is *enough*. How can you possibly sit there and speak so terribly about your father?"

Rachel groaned and got to her feet.

"I'm not quite finished yet," Sam said. He didn't raise his voice, he didn't glare. His tone was simply much more civil, much lower. Much colder.

The look she shot back at Sam could have melted steel, but she resumed her seat.

"Now…" Sam said, his eyes narrowed as if he was losing his patience. "You seem awfully preoccupied with something, Miss James. And it doesn't seem to be your father's funeral."

Rachel folded her arms, choosing once again to look up at the ceiling instead of at us. "It's none of your business," she said.

"I imagine it could be…" Sam said. "Especially if it had something to do with Lucas Adams."

An unexpected chill swept through the room.

Mrs. James near the door gaped at Sam.

Rachel's head snapped toward Sam, her fiery stare becoming at once icy cold. "How do you know that name?" she asked.

"People in this village talk," Sam said slowly, deliberately. "And a little bird told me that you and this Lucas had some sort of relationship?"

Rachel's hard exterior began to crack. Face flushing red, she looked everywhere around the room but at Sam. "We –

we did, but it's been over for some time," she said. "He – he means nothing to me."

"Is that so?" Sam asked, his tone calm and cool. "Then why are you so suddenly flustered, Miss James?"

I had to commend Inspector Graves for his ability to get right to the heart of the issue. In one statement, one mention of a name, he had completely shifted the conversation.

She wrung her hands the same way her mother had, though with a great deal more anger.

"Fine!" she snapped eventually. "Fine..."

I gave Sam a sidelong look.

*Finally...*I thought. *She cracked rather easily, considering how obstinate she was before.*

"What can you tell me about Mr. Adams?" Sam asked.

"I really haven't spoken to him for some time..." Rachel said. "Except...well, he sent me a letter a few days before my father died, asking if we could meet. I had been trying hard to forget about him, since my father was so insistent that we stop seeing one another, and he would have known if I had gone to see Lucas..."

"You seem very bitter about what happened," Sam said.

"Of course I am," she said, wrapping her arms tightly around herself. "I love Lucas, and he loves me...which he so marvelously reminded me of the other day when I saw him..."

Mrs. James closed her eyes, turning her face away. Clearly, this was not news she wanted to hear, either.

"Why do you sound so upset that he told you how he felt?" I asked.

Rachel looked up at me, and I saw her eyes were rimmed

with tears. "Because..." she said. "Because the fool decided it was best to go off to war."

My eyes widened, and I looked over at Sam. *Go to war? Was it to get away from murdering Mr. James?*

"Why?" asked Sam, who seemed to be thinking along the same lines I was. "What does he have to gain by enlisting?"

"I have no idea," Rachel said, her voice cracking. "It's ridiculous, though. He could be killed. Doesn't he know that?"

"I'm sure he must," Sam said. "That's not a small decision."

Rachel clicked her tongue in disgust. "What really bothers me, though, is that he told me he is doing it to get away from me. From the memory of me. Since we can't be together..."

Sam exhaled long and slow through his nose. "I see," he said. "And he told you all this before your father died?"

Rachel nodded her head. "Oh, I could have *screamed* at my father. I have never been so angry at him in my whole life. Pushing a man to enlist just because he was afraid to be around me?"

"Joining up is an honorable decision," Sam said.

"Not when he is using it as an excuse to flee," Rachel said. "I told my father...I told him I blamed him for it all. For my heartbreak, for my unhappiness – "

"Rachel, that's enough," Mrs. James said, but her voice shook as well.

Rachel got to her feet, hands balled into fists. "I'm sorry, Inspector, but I cannot help you find the person who killed my father, because I have no idea who it could be. If you could leave me to my grief, I would very much appreciate it."

With that, she strode from the room, and Sam did nothing to stop her.

Mrs. James followed Rachel with her eyes for a moment. "Rachel, just wait one moment..."

The sound of two sets of footsteps climbing the stairs faded away.

Sam looked at me, his shoulders relaxing. "Well, I never would have considered it, but now I think we have two suspects..."

"Lucas and Rachel?" I asked.

"Anger like that could lead to a crime of passion," Sam said. "Her love for Adams may have been enough to push her over the edge."

"But to kill her father?" I asked.

He shrugged. "I've seen people do worse out of anger."

I swallowed hard. "Well...now what?"

"We go listen to the other side of the story..." Sam said. "See if Rachel would really have had it in her to kill her own father. And sometimes that truth can only be uncovered by speaking to someone on the outside."

12

This investigation was a bit like watching a fox chase a chicken through a field. Chaotic, frightening, and yet, I found I couldn't take my eyes away.

What was so fascinating about murder to humans? It was something so horrific, and yet we couldn't help but feel curious about it.

Maybe it wasn't the curiosity that kept drawing me back. Instead, it was the desire to set things straight, especially when I had lived for so long without any sort of justice or answers for the problems in my own life. I wanted resolution, yet found none. I never wanted anyone to feel that way about anything.

"What do you think the chances are of Rachel really being the one to have killed her father?" I asked Sam as we drove toward Lucas Adams' autobody shop.

"We'll know once we speak to Lucas," Sam said. "They both seem far more viable as suspects then you ever were."

"Thank you," I said, and I meant it. "I wish these situations weren't always so murky."

"As do I," Sam said. "It would have saved me a great deal of stress over the years."

The autobody shop seemed quieter than when I had visited. The number of cars in the drive had decreased; there was one lonely vehicle, which looked recently waxed and shined, beautiful in the morning sunlight that bounced off the chrome accents and the immaculately clean front windscreen.

"He may very well recognize me," I said. "I came here in disguise just a few days ago, after all."

"I'm certain he won't be able to deny the two of us our questions," Sam said. "Especially when we make it known that he and the girl he loved may very well be suspects in this case."

I was very glad in that moment that I was not Lucas Adams.

We made our way inside the shop, and the same upbeat jazz music greeted us from the garage. Sam strode over to the door, peering outside. "Lucas Adams?" he called, his voice carrying over the din.

The young man's head appeared over the top of a car's red bonnet, his face partially obscured by a pair of thick, leather-wrapped goggles.

"Yes, how can I help you?" Lucas asked, stepping out around the vehicle, pulling the goggles off his face.

"My name is Inspector Graves," Sam said, somewhat heavily. I imagined he was as tired of playing chase as I was. "And I have some questions for you about Mr. James and his death."

All the color drained from Lucas's face as he stared concernedly up at Sam. "For me? Why?" he asked.

"We understand that you have had some previous

connections to the family," Sam said. "Namely with the daughter, Rachel James."

Lucas took a step backward. "Y – Yes, I was in a relationship with her, at one point..." he said. "But Mr. James took me aside one evening, and he told me quite clearly that he did not want me to be with his daughter."

That was a rather simple, yet very honest answer, I thought. *Why couldn't he just tell me this before?*

Sam nodded, pinching his lips together. "I imagine that made you quite upset," Sam said.

"Well, yes, of course it did," Lucas said. "I love Rachel, very dearly. But...I have far too much respect for Mr. James not to keep my distance. I'd hoped that keeping myself out of Rachel's life would make my choice easier, but instead, it only made me pine for her more...and so, I've decided to remove myself from the picture for good." His face was set in a look of firm determination. "I've enlisted in the military, and I'm to leave for training soon."

Sam rubbed his chin. "I have two minds about you leaving for the war, son," he said. "One, I think it's honorable, and if you feel that it's best to keep Rachel's father's wishes, even now that he is gone, then I think you should be able to do just that. Perhaps things will be different when you return. However..." he laid a hand on Lucas's shoulder. "The other part of me wonders if you mean to run away because you were the one, in fact...who killed the vicar in the first place."

Lucas looked as if he'd swallowed a stone. "Me? Kill Mr. James?" he asked. "N – no, I would never. Of course, I was upset with his choice, but I never would have – never even *thought* about – "

Sam loosened his grip on the young man. "All right, all

right. I believe you. I've been at this job long enough to know when someone's lying," he said. "What about Rachel?" he asked, his eyes narrowing. "Would she ever be capable of something like that?"

Lucas looked even more disgusted than before. "Absolutely not," he said. "She may have been furious with her father for keeping us apart, and they may not have seen eye to eye on many things...but she did love him, and longed for his acceptance. If I know her, she will be bitter over not being able to make peace with him before he died."

"That would certainly explain her attitude..." I said in a low voice behind Sam.

Sam nodded. "When do you leave for basic training, son?" he asked.

"In about three weeks," Lucas said. "And then I likely won't be back for a long while.

Sam glanced over his shoulder at me. "That means we have three weeks to solve this for sure," he said. He looked back at Lucas. "Stay in Brookminster until I call and let you know this has all been resolved. As a suspect, I cannot let you leave town."

Lucas nodded firmly. "Yes, sir. You can count on me."

Sam and I left the shop a few minutes later.

Sam lingered outside the door, staring at something in the far distance.

"What's the matter?" I asked.

He shook his head. "He's not lying," he said. "He really did respect Mr. James. He may be angry about the situation, but he doesn't have it in him to commit murder."

"And Rachel?" I asked.

Sam shrugged. "Lucas seems to think that she's innocent, too. And I'm inclined to believe him when he says that she wouldn't have done it. He looked me straight in the eye with every word he spoke."

I sighed, leaning against the car. "Where does this leave our investigation, then?" I asked. "We're back at square one if we rule them both out."

Sam shrugged his shoulders, his keys jingling as he pulled them from his pocket. "Indeed, it seems we are. Unfortunately, this is how most of these cases go. We are just going to have to be patient."

"How?" I asked. "This means my name will be back at the top of the suspect list."

"No," Sam said, glaring at me over the top of the car. "No, that's not what it means. We just need to go back to the beginning, retrace the steps already examined, and we will find the answers. I promise you."

"And what if we don't?" I asked. "What if we find nothing, and my name is never cleared? Doesn't that happen sometimes? The murderer gets away?"

Sam's jaw tightened, but he met my gaze with a level, blue one. "It does happen, yes," he said, regret coating his words. "But that doesn't mean it will this time."

I yanked the door open, crawling inside, exasperated.

He was not far behind.

"What about the autopsy?" I asked as we started off back toward the center of the village. "Did that reveal anything interesting?"

Sam said, "Now that you mention it, I haven't received the report yet. Perhaps it will be finished today. That's good thinking, Mrs. Lightholder."

I agreed to go into the station with him, under the same pretense that I was Nathanial's cousin Penelope, in from London. When we arrived, I was astounded that no one seemed to see past my weak disguise. Maybe nobody there had ever looked too closely at my face before.

"Did the coroner come in today?" Sam asked at the receptionist's desk before we walked away.

"He did, yes, and the report is on your desk," she said.

It was amazing how kind the woman could be when she didn't recognize me.

"Thank you," Sam said, and we turned and started toward his office.

He closed the door behind us, and I peeled off my coat and hat, eager for some fresh air. "What does it say?" I asked.

Sam glared at me over his desk. "How would I know? I haven't even opened the file yet."

I blushed, and took a seat across from him. "My apologies," I said, brushing some of my now red hair from my cheeks.

Sam regarded me over the top of the file, his eyes narrowing. "You know...I think I prefer you brunette," he said.

The color in my face deepened as his eyes landed back on the page in his hands.

"...yes, all right..." he muttered under his breath. "...time of day, yes, evening, I know...Ah, here it is."

He placed the file on the desk, spinning it so that I might see it as well. He pressed his finger to a diagram of a long, thin knife that looked as if it had been sketched by hand, out of speculation.

"This must be similar to whatever it was that killed him," Sam said.

"That's a very odd shaped knife, isn't it?" I asked, peering up at him. "Who would have such a thing?"

Sam rubbed his jaw, studying the image. "I'm not certain. It says here that the wound itself was clean, as though the blade was double-edged. Not only that, but the weapon was so long that it was able to puncture completely through his right lung, almost all the way to his back."

"That's no ordinary kitchen knife," I said, my stomach churning.

"No, it certainly is not," Sam said. "It makes me wonder...it's thin enough, that it could have been some sort of combat knife, perhaps one used in the last war."

My stomach dropped. "A soldier's weapon?"

Sam's brow knit together. "It's not as farfetched as it sounds. There are plenty of veterans here in the village," he said. "And it's possible that some of their weapons could still be around somewhere."

He pulled the case file back toward himself. "Yes, this knife is the answer. I think it will be the key to solving this whole thing."

"I guess we will need to ask Rachel James or Lucas Adams about it..." I said.

But then my stomach twisted.

"Wait..." I said, staring up at Sam. "The old man..."

"What old man?" he asked.

"The one who lives near the church," I reminded him impatiently. "He's probably too old to have served in the last war...He must be seventy or more. But perhaps he had a son in the fighting, or someone who brought him back a few things...I've always felt there was something suspicious about him."

Sam's brow furrowed. "There's nothing wrong with following a hunch," he said. "But it's going to require more than a vague suspicion for me to bring him down here for questioning."

"Leave that to me," I said. "You talk to Rachel and Lucas." I snatched my jacket and hat off the back of the chair. "I'll speak to the man again."

"Just be careful, Helen," Sam said, sounding somewhat exasperated. "Every time you go digging for information, you seem to get more than you bargained for."

"I know," I said. "I'll be careful this time."

13

The elderly man was all I could think about as I left the police station.

I made my way back to the Driscoll's house, where Irene and Nathanial were waiting for me to explain what had occurred during my day.

"We didn't find any answers," I said. "Except to learn that we don't think Rachel James or Lucas Adams are the ones who killed Mr. James."

"So where does that leave you?" Irene asked, her brow furrowing.

"With few options," I said. "I told Sam I was going to go and investigate one of our other leads this evening."

"What lead might that be?" Nathanial asked.

"I...I shouldn't tell you," I said. "Things are becoming quite sticky, and Inspector Graves is the only one, aside from you two, who believes in my innocence. If any other policemen come around here looking for me, I would rather you didn't know anything, so you aren't involved."

"But – " Irene said.

"No," I said. "It's better this way. But don't worry. I'm just going to go do a little bit of looking, and then I'll come back. All right? Please don't wait up for me. I'll explain everything in the morning."

Nathanial and Irene exchanged nervous looks.

"Just be careful," Irene said. "Please?"

"I will," I said.

I waited until nightfall, even until Irene and Nathanial retired for the night.

Nothing good happens after midnight...I heard my father saying in my mind. He was adamant that people made their choices during the day. He wasn't wrong. It was the time when inhibitions were lost, and violent things happened.

I dressed in dark colors, donning comfortable shoes that I could walk in without making much noise, and did my best to tie my newly cut hair back. It was a chore, as it was just short enough to not want to stay in the clip I wrestled it into.

Regardless, I departed the Driscoll's home, making my way into the night.

Brookminster was almost entirely silent. Families were tucked into their beds, and dogs were lying faithfully at the ends of those beds, dreaming of chasing squirrels and the postman.

The only sounds were the crickets humming as the final days of summer came to a close. The streetlights glowed warmly, but I did my best to avoid their pools of light, keeping to the shadows instead.

Are you here, Roger? I wondered. *Are you out here tonight with me, watching me like you always seem to be?*

The idea of him keeping an eye on me gave me courage to keep my focus, moving ever closer to Mr. Grey's home.

The church appeared as I reached the center of the village, cresting the top of the hill where it sat. Across the street, tucked away between two other homes, was the shabby cottage that belonged to Mr. Barty Grey.

I wished I knew if he was home or not, and if he was a light sleeper or not.

He's elderly, so he is likely home, I thought, standing across the street in a patch of shadows, staring at the house. *And given the same reasoning, he is likely a light sleeper. Am I even capable of breaking in without him noticing?*

I couldn't believe I was attempting this, but I had no choice. Time was truly running out, and it was now or never. And never was not an option right now.

I took a steadying breath, and started across the street toward his house, steeling my nerves.

How would Roger handle this? I thought as I stopped at the low, stone wall around the house. *Would he go through a window? Or would he try the door?*

My heart pounded in my head as I debated between the two options. How was I going to explain myself if the old man found me?

I hopped the low wall easily, without making much of a sound. I hunched down behind the wall, not wanting any stray passersby to see me.

Maybe I should check around the back of the house, I thought, glancing over my shoulder as I started toward the garden, keeping low to the ground.

Twigs snapped under my feet, making me stop in my tracks, my heart beating so fast it ached. Pausing to look around, I waited for someone to appear, to chase me, to yell out and stop me.

When I reached the back of the garden, I noticed a

thicket of trees pressing up against a narrow strip of grass, which was filled with as much clutter as the front yard. I also noticed a cellar built into the house itself, which was closed up with metal doors.

A bomb shelter? I wondered. *That might be a safer place to check first.*

Approaching the doors, I held my breath, not wanting to be caught.

Reaching out for the door, I tugged, and was surprised when it gave easily.

The gaping hole revealed beneath was a vast depth of shadows. I couldn't see past the third stair leading down.

I swallowed hard, set the door down gently on the grass, and started down the stairs.

On the fourth stair, as my body felt as if it was being absorbed by the shadows themselves, my foot struck something glass, causing it to clatter against the stair.

I groped around with my fingers, and hope sparked within me.

A lantern!

With a few twists of the metal dial set into the base, a flame flickered into life.

There isn't much oil in here, I noticed. *I need to move quickly.*

The light helped guide me down to the base of the stairs, where I found myself in a cool, damp stone cellar. The ceiling was low, the walls moist with trickling water, and a smell of mold hung in the air, making it hard to breathe.

I held the lantern up above my head, looking around the room.

It wasn't a large cellar, but it looked as if it was set up for a secondary home. A low cot with a stained, thin mattress was in one corner, and a metal chest stood in front of it. Shelves lined the wall on either side of another staircase, likely leading to the rest of the house, stocked with preserved foods and other necessaries like blankets and jugs of water. Boxes were stacked and carefully labeled.

*Such a difference from the front yard...*I realized, walking further into the room. *He must really take his doomsday preparations seriously.*

I set the lantern down on the table beside the bed, wandering over to the shelves to examine the contents more closely.

It didn't take long for me to realize that there was nothing special or out of the ordinary there.

I glanced over my shoulder at the metal chest that stood at the foot of the dirty, rusted cot. My heart skipped. If anything questionable were to be hidden somewhere...

I walked over to it, kneeling down in front of it, and lifted the lid.

I gasped, falling back onto my hands, my stomach twisting into knots.

A long, narrow knife rested atop a towel just inside, almost a perfect match to the blade that the coroner had drawn on the autopsy report he had given Sam.

It was pristine, shining in the light of the lantern, as if it had been recently polished.

*Which would make sense, if it was recently used to kill the vicar...*I thought.

I looked around, and war trophies began to reveal themselves to me. A jacket thrown over a chair with patches in the sleeve and pins on the breast pocket, indicating some sort of rank. A flag pinned to the wall behind the stack of boxes. A rifle hanging on a peg beside the stairs where I'd entered the bunker. It seemed that I was right about someone having brought him items back from the last war. Either that, or the old man himself had fought in some prior war. I wasn't familiar enough with these items to be certain of their age, but it didn't really matter where they had come from.

I stood, staring down into the chest. This was it. This was the proof I needed.

Barty Grey had been the one to kill Mr. James.

"I should have known there was something suspicious about you..."

A light shone into the dark room, the bright bulb of a flashlight pointed right at my eyes.

I threw up my arm, trying to block the piercing glow making me squint.

Footsteps echoed down the stairwell, leading up into the rest of the house, and I could just make out the silhouette of a man coming to a stop at the bottom.

"You're the one who was snooping around the church the other day, aren't you?" he asked. "Asking all those questions about the vicar, and if I'd seen anything funny..."

I glanced toward the door, wondering if I could make it up there without him catching me.

"So, you are working with the police like I thought?" he asked.

I didn't want to answer. There was no reason why I had to answer him, anyways. If he intended to fight me, trying to talk to him would not change his mind.

"I caught you red handed," he said. "You may as well have been holding that knife you seem so fascinated to have found."

I couldn't tell if he was holding a weapon or anything,

but I knew that I didn't have long to make a decision. He hadn't been the steadiest on his feet, and I was significantly younger than he was. If I made a run for it...

"What, cat got your tongue?" Mr. Grey asked, taking another step toward me. "Say something!"

The only thing I heard was the sound of my own blood surging through my ears.

You can do it, I told myself, not even realizing that I'd somehow formulated a plan. *One...two...*

"Hey," Mr. Grey barked, waving the flashlight in my face. "Listen to me when I'm talking to you!"

Without waiting another moment, I wheeled around and snatched the knife from the inside of the metal trunk. In that same breath, I vaulted toward the door, willing my feet to carry me as fast as they possibly could.

"Hey!" Mr. Grey shouted after me as I bolted up the stairs leading back outside. "Get back here!"

I kept the knife close to my chest, careful not to catch it on my clothing or my flesh, as the blade was bare. The cold metal bit through the fabric of my blouse as I ran.

I'd barely made it to the back garden, the coolness of the night stealing the heat from my face, when I heard him tearing up the stairs after me. Was his weakness, his leaning on his cane, all a ruse?

I kept running, having to vault over some boxes strewn about in the side yard, careful to keep my head low and my eyes focused on my escape route.

He was close on my heels, though. I heard him yelling at me, though nothing was clear or coherent.

I needed to get to the police station, but I was going to have to lose him first.

I stared around, my mind working faster than I could register.

Where could I hide? Behind a tree? In the cemetery somewhere?

A light in a window inside the church caught my attention. Who could have been there at this hour?

I chanced a look over my shoulder, and found my pursuer had tripped over some of the rubbish in his front garden.

This is my chance, I thought, and disappeared into the shadows between the street lamps.

"You won't get away from me!" he shouted across the yard, though his voice was strained as he struggled back to his feet. "I – I will catch you!"

Something told me he definitely would if he could untangle himself from whatever it was he'd tripped over. Why had I underestimated him like I had?

I hurried through the gates outside the church, hoping I would be able to make it inside without much trouble. It would be a good place to wait for him to pass.

I tried the door, and was surprised to find it unlocked.

I slipped inside, breathing a sigh of relief.

Perhaps I would be safe. For now.

14

I looked around the church, finding the light that had been switched on coming from Mr. James' old study. Why was that on? Had someone forgotten to turn it off earlier?

As I made my way over to it, I peered inside the small room, and my heart sank.

Boxes were strewn all over the floor, some of which were packed with books or clutter from the desk and shelves. Others were empty, waiting to be filled.

The desk seemed so lonely, with nothing more than a few stray pens on its surface, along with a few copies of the church bulletin...the date on which was the Sunday before Mr. James was killed.

The creak of a door behind me made me turn around, and I found myself staring down Mr. Grey...who carried his rifle, and was pointing it at me.

My stomach dropped to the floor. Why did I keep finding myself in these situations?

"There, now..." he said, kicking the door shut with his

foot. The finality of the *bang* as it slammed shut sent shivers down my spine.

He'd lost the flashlight in our mad dash, so it was easier to see him now. He'd donned his old military jacket, and he clutched his cane, which he was leaning heavily upon.

"You can drop the act," I said, glaring across the space at him. "If you could run after me, you clearly don't need that cane."

"Just because I can chase after you doesn't mean that my old war injuries don't act up," he said. "Now…give me back the knife, and we can both go home and pretend like this whole thing never happened."

"How can I?" I asked. "Not when this clearly proves that you were the one to kill Mr. James."

The old man sighed. "How can you think that?" he asked. "I heard the poor sod was stabbed, but that doesn't mean it was my knife that did it."

"It does when it matches the description in the autopsy report," I said. "And I intend to turn this over to the police for inspection."

There was a flash of danger in Mr. Grey's eyes.

"What is it?" I asked. "If you didn't kill him, then what's the harm in them looking the blade over? Wouldn't it be better to clear your name? Because as I see it right now, you are the only one capable of killing him."

He shook his head. "Young lady, if you understand the sort of life I've lived, you would realize that life and death are really rather subjective. I could be ordered to kill a man who I would never wish to under ordinary circumstances, and then forbidden from raising a hand against someone who deserved it. That's why the battlefield confuses so many when they return home. They have a hard time making the lines clear again."

I gripped the knife tighter. "Are you admitting to the murder? Saying that you think Mr. James deserved his death?"

He adjusted his hold on his rifle, which made me flinch and take a step back.

"Mr. James was a good man," Mr. Grey said. "Really, what happened to him wasn't his fault. His conscience was too strong. That made him dangerous, especially given what he did for a living..."

"What do you mean by that?" I asked.

"It was almost a year ago now. I ended up in a hospital, with some illness that nobody understood. Doctors were convinced I was going to die. So Mr. James came to visit me. He prayed with me and asked me about where I stood with the Lord...In those moments, I realized there were still things I had never admitted, never repented of...and so I shared those things with Mr. James."

"What sort of things?" I asked.

Mr. Grey's face screwed up with anger. "Not the sort of things I would ever tell you," he said.

"Well, you clearly did not perish as you thought you might," I said. "You're still standing here, aren't you?"

The old man nodded. "I am. But after recovering, I realized I never should have shared what I did with the vicar. As I said, the man had a strong conscience, and the things I told him could very well land me in prison if he told anyone else. He might have felt compelled to let the police in on what I'd done."

"But you couldn't let him do that, could you?" I asked, everything finally starting to make sense. "So you decided to take matters into your own hands so that your secrets would never be revealed?"

Mr. Grey looked down at the rifle in his hands, and I heard a distinct *click* as he readied it, pointing it back at me. "That's precisely it," he said. "You're quite the clever one, aren't you?"

I put my hands in the air, keeping his blade flat against my palm, showing him I still had it. There was no way I could reach him with it in time to defend myself...and if I did, that would make it impossible for the police to check and see if there were any traces of Mr. James' blood on the blade.

"If you'd simply kept your nose out of all this, you never would have found yourself in this situation. Like I told you, the lines are blurred, and sometimes we need to make difficult choices in order to survive," he said.

"You're telling me that choosing to kill is still a difficult decision for you?" I asked.

He shrugged. "In a way. But it's happened so often now that I'm fast growing numb to it."

"Why not turn yourself in, then?" I asked. "Take steps toward setting things right."

"That depends on your perspective, I suppose," he said. "In my mind, sending myself to prison is far from right."

He hoisted the rifle to his shoulder, leaning against the wall for support.

My heart raced. How many times was I going to have a gun pointed at me, my life being threatened?

I closed my eyes...and heard a deafening *bang* ring out in the church.

One heartbeat passed.

Then another.

I waited for the pain, waited for my knees to give way, waited to feel the blossoming of the hot, red blood across my chest as it finally registered what had happened.

But none of that ever came.

I opened my eyes and watched as Mr. Grey staggered, his rifle tumbling from his hands...and collapsed to the floor.

Clutching my hand over my racing heart, I looked all around.

My eyes fell on a young woman standing in the front row of pews, a small handgun clasped tightly in her grip, the end of the barrel smoking slightly.

My jaw fell as I realized who it was. "Rachel James?" I breathed.

The young woman didn't move, her eyes fixed on the spot where Mr. Grey had been standing. I watched the rapid rise and fall of her chest. I could see the paleness in her cheeks, even in the dim light.

"I heard everything," she said, her voice shaking. "I came here tonight to make peace with my father's death...and I heard everything that wretched man said..."

I was at her side in a moment, my arms wrapped around her as she tossed the gun aside and collapsed into the pew, her wailing filling the vaulted ceilings high above us.

15

"I think I'm going to buy you a dog," Inspector Graves said, looking down at me. "A big one, and I think I will have to insist that you take him everywhere with you. Because you always seem to find yourself in these terrible situations when you are alone."

I pulled the blanket that had been tossed over my shoulders more tightly around myself, my eyes fixed upward on the stained glass window at the back of the church. "Yes, perhaps that wouldn't be such a bad idea..."

Sam took a seat beside me in the pew.

I didn't want to look behind me. The police had arrived, and were busy tending to the body. I heard the rustle of clothing, the scuff of boots, the murmur of men's voices as they moved the late Mr. Grey's corpse from the floor of the church.

Sam sighed, resting his hands on his knees. "Rachel James will be all right," he said in a gentle tone. "I know it's difficult to see someone as distraught as she was, but it will take time for her to heal. Taking someone's life is...well, you certainly understand."

That I did. Seeing the horror in her eyes made the memory of Sidney's death come back fresh to my mind, and I was doing all I could to keep those thoughts at bay.

"I wish there was something more I could do for her," I said. "She came here to make peace with what happened to her father, to pray about her heartache, and then...well, we showed up, and she overheard it all..."

"But if she hadn't been here, then who knows what would have happened to you?" Sam asked.

"I know very well what would have happened," I said. "He had no qualms about killing me. Didn't even seem troubled by it, honestly. He said those lines were blurred for him when he was in the war."

Sam's face darkened. "I suppose I can understand how he reached that conclusion, as wrong as it is."

I tried to swallow, but my throat was too dry. It felt as if my tongue was made of sandpaper.

"I'm going to have to ask you to consider staying with the Driscolls again for a few nights," Sam said. "I'm worried about you being home alone, after everything that's happened."

"I suppose I could speak with them," I said. "Though I hate to impose any further."

Sam shook his head. "I've already spoken to them. Irene insisted."

"At this rate, I may as well move in with them," I said with a wry laugh.

"Inspector Graves?" I heard behind us.

Sam seemed reluctant to answer, but turned around. "What is it?"

"We need you to finish the report," said one of the officers.

"Very well," he said heavily, getting to his feet. "I'll be back in a moment. Just rest, all right?"

I nodded, watching him walk away.

As I turned my face back toward the altar at the front of the room, I sighed heavily.

It was a few days later that I found myself wandering through the village, feeling free to do so once again. It was surprising how quickly all of my neighbors' ill feeling toward me disappeared once the truth about Mr. James murder became public. I might have received a few strange looks from a person or two, but everyone seemed pleased that I was not the one responsible for the death.

The knife had been analyzed and confirmed as the weapon that had killed the vicar, due to small traces of his blood remaining on the blade.

Rachel James was exonerated and hailed as a hero, but she hadn't been seen in public since that night at the church. I didn't blame her in the least. Her life was going to be difficult for some time, and she was going to need time to learn how to live with the choices she'd made.

As I walked, I passed by the place where I had spotted Roger that one day.

I suddenly remembered the brooch I'd left there, wondering if he'd ever gone back to pick it up.

I wandered into the alleyway, and located the stone I'd written our initials on. It gave easily as I lifted it up off the rest of the others stacked on the wall.

The brooch was gone, to my surprise...and a small, white flower was lying in its place.

My heart skipped as I gently picked it up.

It was a lily...my favorite flower.

Hope swelled within me. There was no doubt in my mind now. It was Roger that was following after me.

I didn't want to hope too much, though. I worried that if I were to open my heart to the possibility of our reconciling, those hopes would only be dashed.

I realized the best thing I could do was be patient, and see what happened between us next. For now, I could be content with these little gifts of affection between the two of us.

I closed my hand carefully over the crushed flower, and replaced the stone.

With a smile tugging at the corner of my mouth, I made my way from the alleyway, back out into the sunshine.

Life was full of difficulties, but what made it worth living were the little moments of happiness that came...some in the form of flowers and hints of affection.

I didn't know where Roger was, or what might happen between us someday...but I did know that he was making a sacrifice for his country, and that his silence was likely intended to protect me.

For now, I could be content with that, and in knowing that despite having to keep the truth from me for so long, he still found a way to let me know he cared.

"Helen, are you ready?"

It was Irene, waving to me from down near the bakery. We were looking for something special for Nathanial's birthday party that evening.

"I'm coming!" I called, and hurried out to greet her, allowing joy to fill my heart once again.

Continue following the mysterious adventures of Helen Lightholder in
"A Simple Country Deception."

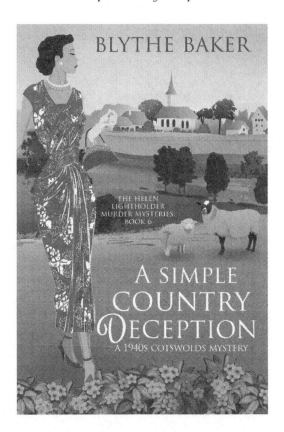

ABOUT THE AUTHOR

Blythe Baker is the lead writer behind several popular historical and paranormal mystery series. When Blythe isn't buried under clues, suspects, and motives, she's acting as chauffeur to her children and head groomer to her household of beloved pets. She enjoys walking her dog, lounging in her backyard hammock, and fiddling with graphic design. She also likes binge-watching mystery shows on TV.

To learn more about Blythe, visit her website and sign up for her newsletter at www.blythebaker.com